BREAKING FREE

CATHRYN FOX

Where reality is whatever you wish it to be…

After you read *Breaking Free* you'll find the bonus story,

HANDS ON with the CEO!

INVITATION TO EDEN

We are very pleased to issue your Invitation to Eden, an exciting series coming to you in 2014 from 27 of the biggest names in romance. Join us as we take you on an exciting adventure to Eden, where anything... and everything goes!

www.InvitationToEden.com

CHAPTER ONE

First week of college.

Alaska Rossi, aka, Janey Smith to all those who knew her at her upstate campus, leaned back in her chair and looked over the five cards in her hand. She tried to concentrate, but it was damn hard to focus on the jacks and aces, considering there were three half-dressed guys and three half-dressed girls—one of those being her—all sitting around the common room table.

Wearing only his jeans, Jordan, one of the buff football players, finished off his beer and pushed to his feet. "I need another brew." He walked to the mini-fridge and pulled the door open. "Anyone else?"

Everyone at the table nodded except Alaska. Glancing at her nearly empty bottle, she shook her head. She wasn't much of a drinker and was feeling the effects of the two beers she'd had already.

"Ah, come on, Janey," Melanie, the pretty blonde sitting across from her said, her voice slurring slightly. "It's our first year of college. We're finally out from under our parents' thumbs, so why not loosen up and have another drink?"

A tremble moved through Alaska. If they only knew. Even though she was thousands of miles away from home, as the daughter of a powerful mob boss, she'd never be out from under her father's thumb. No, even though she rarely saw him, he still had full control over her every moment. Of course, she couldn't tell Melanie that. Here on campus, she was going under an alias, and after a near kidnapping when she was a child—her father's rival wanting to use her to get to him—she knew better than to let anyone get too close.

Trevor sidled closer to her, his eyes zeroing in on the cleavage spilling out from her lacey pink bra. "Yeah, come on, have another one with me," he urged, like he too was interested in loosening her up.

Colin, one of the other football players, cracked his beer open, chugged it, and reached for another. He let loose a loud burp, and Emery giggled, obviously drunk if she found his crudeness attractive.

Alaska shrugged. "All right. Why not? Give me another." Truthfully, she was sick and tired of always being watched over and just wanted to have some fun. Which was exactly why she was barely dressed and playing strip poker with five virtual strangers during her first week on campus.

Jordan handed her a bottle. She twisted off the cap and took a long drink, then laid her cards out. Groans echoed around the table when they saw her full house. Melanie laid her cards down, and when the boys saw that she'd lost, they started chanting, "Take it off, take it off."

Grinning, Melanie peeled her bra off, and the guys practically drooled when her breasts fell free. She jiggled them, and her glance caught Jordan's.

"Eat your hearts out boys," she cooed.

"I plan on eating something out," Jordan mumbled.

As he shifted uncomfortably and adjusted his pants, Melanie bit her lip in a playful, seductive manner. Clearly, those two would be hooking up tonight.

Alaska pushed back a twinge of envy for the two of them. How wonderful to be free, to throw caution to the wind, casually pick out a guy, and hook up with him. She peeked up at the other guys in the game and considered which one she'd like to take back to her room. But as she looked at them, she couldn't help but think about Jesse Cavanaugh, the dorm's hot resident assistant. She'd met him last week when she moved in, and since he lived two doors down, she'd had the good fortune to run into him on a daily basis. Hot, hard, and rough around the edges, everything about Jesse screamed sex and had her body reacting with need whenever he was around—and even when he wasn't. There was just something about him that held her attention and, quite frankly, fascinated her.

Jordan leaned back in his chair, and the legs teetered. "Whoa," he yelled and damn near fell over. As the guys all laughed, Alaska picked up the cards, shuffled, and dealt another round. She cringed when she saw the mish mash in her hand.

"Great poker face you got there, Janey," Trevor said, his leg rubbing up against hers under the table.

She grabbed her beer and took a big drink, her brain growing fuzzier around the edges. She tossed four cards away and dealt a second round. If she didn't get something decent this time around, she'd be the next one going topless. As she envisioned herself removing her bra in front of all these people, a strange new tingling zipped through her blood.

Honestly, she'd never done anything quite so naughty before, but had to admit, it secretly thrilled her. God, who knew she had exhibition tendencies? Certainly not her, since she'd been kept sheltered her entire life. Then again, she did love reading about it.

Colin adjusted his cards. "Hell yeah!" he said, fisting one hand in triumph. "Looks like I'm about to see me some more titties."

To Alaska's left, Emery put her finger to her lips and giggled. "Quiet you guys, or Jesse will hear us and shut down this game."

"Fuck Jesse," Trevor said.

Fuck Jesse, indeed.

Warmth grew between Alaska's legs, and she squirmed as that delicious scenario played out in her mind's eye.

Everyone laid their cards out, and Trevor looked at hers. He grinned, pointed to her bra, and said, "Take it off, baby."

Feeling a bubble of excitement well up inside her, Alaska slipped the straps off her shoulder and slowly drew them down before unhooking it from the back. She let it drop to the floor with the rest of her clothes.

Jordan whistled and leaned back further in his chair, but this time, the legs did give out. He toppled over, his beer spilling all over the tile floor. As he let loose a loud curse, laughter broke out again.

Melanie jumped up to help him, but her feet went out from underneath her on the wet surface. She rocked the table, and everyone's bottles toppled over. Alaska pushed back in her chair, but not before the cold beer spilled into her lap. In all the commotion, Melanie landed on Jordan with a thump, and his curse turned into a moan when her breasts settled over his face.

"What the hell is going on here?"

Collective gasps could be heard in the room as all eyes turned toward the door.

The second Alaska saw Jesse standing there, his eyes dropping to her near naked body, desire slammed into her like a sonic boom. She took a breath but could barely fill her lungs as those piercing blue eyes moved over her, leaving her feeling breathless, hot...so needy for his touch.

In a blur of activity, Colin grabbed Emery's hand, and Jordan grabbed Melanie's. They bolted from the room, leaving her there with Trevor and Jesse.

Jesse turned to Trevor and took a combat stance as Trevor climbed from his seat and squared off against him.

"Beat it," Jesse said, jerking his thumb toward the door behind him.

As Trevor stood there sizing up his opponent, he had a moment of hesitation. While Trevor was built and buff, his body and muscles lacked Jesse's sinewy definition. Couple that with the scars on his face, and anyone with half a brain knew Jesse wasn't a guy to mess with.

Trevor backed down and mumbled something about his football scholarship as he slinked past Jesse. When Jesse turned back to Alaska, taking in her near nakedness a second time, she felt her nipples harden and her pussy grow moist.

She listened to his throat work as he swallowed and knew this was her chance to seduce the guy she'd been fantasizing about all week. She blinked, working to clear her foggy head while she kicked herself for having that third drink.

"Let's go," Jesse said, scrubbing his chin.

She stood up, her heavy breasts on full display. "Where?"

"You...uh..." He exhaled slowly and pointed to the heap on the floor. "Your clothes."

"I can get them tomorrow."

The muscles along his jaw rippled, and he rooted his feet. "Or you can get them now."

"Fine." She bent down to get them, but a wave of dizziness overcame her. The next thing she knew, she was in Jesse's arms. As his warm scent washed over her, her body moistened and she wondered if he could smell her excitement.

"Are you okay?" he asked, his voice sounding a little more hoarse then before.

"I am now." She wrapped her hands around his neck, her nipples so hard, so desperate for attention, a moan caught in her throat.

"I think I need to get you to bed."

She smiled. Yes! After a week of fantasizing about him, Jesse was finally going to give her what she wanted. Her mind traveled an erotic path as he carried her down the hall. She writhed slightly as she pictured him touching her body, his tongue licking the nub that was swelling painfully between her legs.

"Mmmm," she moaned as she put her mouth on his neck, stealing a taste of his skin.

He shifted her in his arms and turned her doorknob, then he used his shoulder to nudge it open. With nothing but the moonlight shining in from the slant in her curtains, he carried her to her bed. Her insides shook and her body pulsed, so eager to feel his naked skin nest to hers. He lowered her onto her mattress, his fingers skimming over her flesh as he covered her with a blanket.

"Jesse..." she murmured, swiping her tongue over her bottom lip. She reached for him, but he backed up. Wait, what? What was going on?

"You need sleep."

She shook her head. "No, I need you," she murmured.

He raked his hand through his disheveled hair. "I gotta go."

What the hell? Here she was, all but naked, her entire body beckoning his touch, and he was just going to walk away. What kind of guy walked away from a sure thing?

She blinked, her fuzzy mind trying to sort through matters.

"Get some sleep, Ala…uh…Janey."

With that, he disappeared through her door. As it clicked shut behind him, and she tried to part the fog clouding her thoughts, she suddenly jackknifed in her bed.

Wait, was he just about to call her Alaska?

* * *

Jesse paced his room, his cock so goddamn hard he was about to shoot off in his pants. How he was going to watch over Alaska—or rather Janey Smith—for the next year without helping himself to a taste was beyond him.

From the pictures he saw at her father's place, he knew she was gorgeous, but seeing her up close and personal was another matter altogether.

And those breasts…fuck.

When she writhed in his arms, her body so hot and needy, it took every ounce of strength he had not to take her up on her invitation. But it wasn't just her sexy body that caught his attention. Oh no, not at all. After watching her steadily for a week now and seeing the quiet reflective side to her when she was alone, not to mention the untamed spirit in her when she danced, he couldn't help but feel drawn to her. There was a real sweetness about her, a kindness and honesty that he rarely saw in others. He also saw a loneliness that he could relate to. It made him want to take her into his arms and tell her everything would be okay.

He threw himself on his unmade sheets and stared at his clock. After tossing and turning for what felt like hours, he rolled out of bed, deciding a cold shower was in order. He opened his door, and as night settled over the dorm, he was greeted with quiet. Without bothering to turn on the hallway lights, he made his way down the corridor.

When he reached the common bathroom—the boys and girls shower area separated only by a bank of shared sinks—he heard a strange noise. His footsteps slowed, and he listened. The noise, a mix between a moan and a strangled cry, sounded again, and this time he could tell it was coming from the female shower area.

When it grew louder, unease moved through him. Was someone hurt? Since it was his job to oversee the floor, he quietly walked around the tall partition wall.

"Hello," he called out, but his words were met with more cries.

Moving a little quicker, he hurried toward the commotion, and what he saw next stole the breath from his lung.

Alaska...

He took in the look on her face, the honesty and openness she displayed as she aimed the nozzle head between her legs. She touched herself, her fingers slicking over her hot button, one his mouth was watering to taste.

Her full lips parted, and she made a sexy bedroom noise as she brought herself to orgasm. His cock instantly hardened, and there was nothing he could do to stifle the moan crawling out of his throat. The sound gained her attention. Startled, her lids flicked open, but when she saw it was him, heat moved into her eyes.

Walk away, Jesse. Just walk away.

He took a distancing step back, knowing better than to cross that line. She was sweet and sexy, and not only would her bastard father kill him if he so much as touched her, everything in his gut warned that he could get in deep with a girl like her. And the truth was, Alaska deserved someone better than him in her life. He took another step back, but when he saw the disappointment on her face, the need in her eyes, it felt like a physical blow to the gut.

He wasn't sure why, but there was something about her that made him want to take care of her, to protect her, to give her everything she'd ever wanted. The one thing he did know, however, was that it had nothing to do with being her hired bodyguard.

CHAPTER TWO

Spring Break: six months later.

Feeling horribly sorry for herself, Alaska let loose an exaggerated breath and snatched her floral cosmetic bag off the small bedside table. Since everyone in her residence was down south partying during Spring Break, and she had nothing to keep her occupied on this cold Chicago night, she decided to grab a long, hot shower and climb into bed early. At least between the sheets she'd have something to do, like read one of her favorite Sarah Fawkes or Eliza Gayle books, a nice prelude to stroking her needy body and bringing herself to orgasm while she fantasized about her dorm's hot residence assistant.

Or at least the guy who was masquerading as their floor's RA.

As she thought about Jesse Callaghan, the tough biker boy who resided two doors down and always smelled like warm leather, hot sex, and motorcycle fumes, she knew there was more to him than met the eye. Everything from the way he took care of her that night when he caught her half naked playing poker—when most guys would have taken advantage of the situation—to how he *always* watched her, told her he was no ordinary college boy.

Not at all.

After seeing him every day, watching the way he moved and acted, everything in her gut told her Jesse was a guy who'd been dragged up on the streets, his homegrown muscles a product of survival, not some polished, overpriced gym. And he was here masquerading as the floor's RA, for one reason and one reason only.

Her.

All things considered, including the night when he almost let her real name slip from his lips, she knew he had to be one of her father's men. Even though it pissed her off that her father had gone behind her back and secretly hired Jesse to watch over her, there was no denying that biker boy was still nice to look at, and even nicer to fantasize about. Since Alaska had very few acquaintances on campus, and life here was as vanilla and uninspiring as her alias, at least her badass bodyguard gave her something other than her assignments to occupy her mind at night. She didn't bother to call him on it. There was no point, really. Plus, she didn't want to take a chance that her father would replace him with someone else, someone not quite so…yummy.

She took a moment to imagine what it would be like to peel that worn leather jacket from his broad shoulders, to touch that hard body all over with her fingers, her mouth, her tongue. As a fine shiver of want traveled the length of her spine, she tucked her cosmetic bag under her arm, grabbed a fluffy cotton towel from her closet, and used her shoulder to push through her dorm room door. She pulled it shut behind her, and the old hinges groaned like a wounded animal and cut through the unnatural silence in the hallway before the lock clicked into place.

She stepped into the long corridor and followed the dim path leading to the shower area. The coldness of the tile seeped into her bare feet, and as the blackness in the hall enveloped her, her thoughts once again returned to her father and how distant he was with her. But thinking of him instantly darkened her mood and stirred the sense of loneliness that had long ago taken up residence inside of her.

She hated how little he had to do with her, how easily he dismissed her, sending her to an out of state college and insisting she earn a business degree—no doubt so she could help cook the books when she returned home. Except accounting was the last thing she wanted to do.

Truthfully, she wanted to be a dancer, a performer of sorts, but the man she called daddy—when he happened to be around—cared nothing about her wants or needs. No, the man who didn't deserve the title of father, the man who had wanted a son, not a daughter, cared only about what was best for him. And it wasn't like she had a mother to turn to. Marilyn Rossi had skipped town years ago, never to be heard from again. As a child, her disappearance had hurt deeply, but as Alaska grew older, she realized that any mother who would abandon her little girl and leave her with a man who was as cold as the snow covered streets outside her window wasn't someone Alaska wanted around anyway.

Sure, her father had secretly hired a bodyguard to detail her every move, but she knew it was his way of shielding himself. The man had enemies, so if Jesse was watching out for her, then no one could get to the all-powerful and mighty Franco Rossi through his one and only offspring.

If only she could get out from under his control, go

somewhere where she could simply be Alaska Rossi. Although she honestly had no idea who that girl really was, considering she'd never been given the opportunity to really find herself.

Not wanting to dwell on those disheartening thoughts any longer, she padded quietly down the empty hall. She had only taken a few steps when a familiar sensation came over her. Slowing her pace, she angled her head and held her breath, straining her ears for some telltale sound in the darkness. She stole a glance over her shoulder, half expecting to find Jesse lingering in the distance, watching her with those hard, piercing eyes of his. Her body stirred to life, and warmth invaded her nether region as she thought about the intense way he watched her. He reminded her of a predatory animal, patiently watching its prey, waiting for the right moment to pounce and claim its prize. The thought of being claimed by him brought heat to the valley between her thighs and had her thoughts careening in an erotic direction.

She searched the hall, but when her glance came up empty, the vixen inside her wondered where her bodyguard was hiding tonight and what it would actually take to get him to act on the heat between them.

She stepped into the common area. Since modern dorms had little privacy, the area housed a big mirror and dozens of sinks where both guys and girls could attend to their hygiene simultaneously. To the left, behind a high partitioning wall, the girls shower area awaited her. The same set-up could be found to her right, where a 'boys only' sign went ignored. While she'd never personally broken that rule, she knew many girls who showered with the guys, two or three at a time, actually. A strange quiver moved through her as she visualized that delicious scenario. Of course, the 'girls only' sign also went unheeded. Many guys crossed over into female territory, but unfortunately, none had ever come looking for her. Then again, Jesse had crossed it that night six months ago when she was alone in one of the open stalls, deep under the hot spray, utilizing the shower nozzle in the most creative ways.

His reactions told her he'd wanted her, but unfortunately, he clearly had no intentions of doing anything about it.

She was about to turn to the girls showers when the scent of leather wafted before her nose. She inhaled, pulling the arousing aroma deep into her lungs as she listened to the water turn on in the guy's section. Her heart went into her throat, because she knew there was only one guy left in residence this week. Only one guy who could be naked, merely a few feet away from her needy body.

Jesse.

Her flesh warmed all over as she visualized him under that spray, hot water dripping down his rock hard body. She spotted his towel draped over one of the sinks, and because severe boredom was messing with her mind, a naughty idea began to formulate. Hell, if she couldn't have any fun down south with the rest of her dorm mates, then maybe she could get into a little mischief here on campus. It was juvenile and inappropriate, she knew, but hey, every now and then, a girl's gotta have a little fun, right?

Without thinking her plan through, she grabbed his towel, threw it over her shoulder, and backed out of the room, all the while telling herself this was simply payback. Biker Boy always kept a measure of distance with her, even when she blatantly tried to seduce him. Forcing him to walk back to his room sans towel was simply her way of getting back at him for not treating her as anything more than a school kid under his care.

As she retraced her steps and once again found

herself in the hall, the provocative mental image of a naked Jesse making his way from the shower to his room twisted her insides. She took a moment to recall how hot he looked in his jeans, how he filled them out in all the right places. Her body trembled and fueled the need inside her. Okay, she seriously needed to get laid.

It had been far too long since a guy had touched her, *really* touched her. It would feel so good to know a guy's hands were on her because he wanted her, not just using her to get closer to her father. But Jesse kept a cool exterior that she doubted even her father's toughest henchman could crack.

As steam spilled out into the hallway, she blew a wispy strand of hair from her face and took a moment to think about what it would take to break the boy who held his control close. What it would take to feel those callused palms of his on her breasts, between her legs. She could only imagine those hands could rev up a woman with the same skill and speed they revved up that high performance motorcycle of his.

Desire moved through her as she carefully made her way down the hall. But when she caught his scent on the towel, her steps slowed, ribbons of guilt twisting in the pit of her stomach. She passed his closed bedroom and puckered her lips in thought as she ran her hands over the warm terry cloth. While her lascivious brain took that moment to entertain the idea of him exiting the shower buck naked, there was a part of her that couldn't help but take a moment to consider his predicament.

Jesse probably hated being on campus as much as she did. Sitting in lecture halls and being forced to take accounting classes probably bored the living hell out of him, too. But because he was young and hot, and no doubt the only guy in her father's arsenal who could pull off the ruse, he found himself forced to babysit a mobster's daughter. She of all people knew he could never refuse the assignment, because once under the control of Franco Rossi, always under his control. The only way any of her father's men got out from his strong hold was in a body bag, which meant Jesse was as much of a prisoner as she was.

Guilt eating at her, she turned, intent on putting the towel back. Jesse didn't deserve this from her, but before she could take a step, she came face-to-face, or rather face-to-chest, with the hottest guy she'd ever set eyes on. Anger flashed in his baby blues as they locked with hers.

At least, she thought it was anger.

"I...uh..." she began around a tongue gone thick. He slicked his hair off his forehead, accentuating the scars on his face. Her eyes moved over the age-old wounds that added to his ruggedness and good looks.

Unable to hold his gaze any longer, her eyes dropped. Coherent thought fled when she glimpsed his gorgeous, naked body, specifically, the impressive cock between his legs, which, the longer she looked, began to harden. As she registered every delicious inch of him, her gaze followed the tattoo scrolls on his arms. A strange wheezing sound escaped her throat as she took a moment to admire the swirls, trying to figure out what they meant. Flustered, she struggled for words. But how could she form a sentence when all she could think about was touching the naked man before her?

Oh Gawd...

Okay, so she'd set out to take his towel as payback, a childish act of rebellion, yet as she salivated over his hard, wet body—one, she fully understood, he wasn't about to ever let her touch—she couldn't help but think she was the one actually being punished.

* * *

Sweet Jesus.

Alaska was going to be the fucking death of him yet.

Jesse took a distancing step back and bit down on his jaw hard enough to break bone. Desperate for something constructive to do with his hands before they got him into trouble, he ran his fingers through his wet hair and worked to marshal his cock. But how was he supposed to tame his dick when Alaska was tracking his body with those dark, sexy bedroom eyes of hers? As they stood there staring at each other like they were in the middle of some goddamn Mexican standoff, he shifted restlessly and wondered who was going to make the first move, and more importantly, what that move might be.

When her glance met his again, she blinked thick lashes over come-hither eyes, ones that not only told him she needed so much, but exactly who she needed it from. His glance left her face, and he couldn't help but notice the telltale hardening of her nipples beneath the oversize night shirt she wore. He stifled a groan of want as he visualized himself ripping that thin piece of material from her body to expose the ripe, innocent girl beneath, one who'd been beckoning his touch in the most mind-fucking ways. He swallowed, and despite his best interest, let his glance dip lower. *Fuck...* He tugged on his hair harder as his brain conjured the path his hands wanted take. As his gaze visually caressed her curves, he couldn't help but wonder what it would be like to watch the stifled girl before him blossom beneath his touch.

She was speaking, but damned if he could decipher her words, not when the blood in his body was pooling in his groin region. His gaze moved back to her face, and he watched her mouth, trying to figure out what she was saying, but when she nibbled her bottom lip, his cock grew another inch. Christ, how could such an innocent gesture be so sexy?

"...a towel?" she said.

"What?" he murmured, working to get himself under control before he did something he could only regret later, like pin her against that wall and give her what she so obviously wanted…what they've both wanted for a long time now.

"I…uh… I didn't realize anyone was in the shower. I thought I was alone here and—"

"Janey."

"Yeah?" she said, breathlessly.

He cleared his throat and nodded toward her outstretched arm. "Toss it," he ordered, knowing better than to take a step closer to grab it himself. Fuck, if she was within arm's reach, there was no way he could be held accountable for what he did next.

She threw it his way. He snatched it out of the air before it hit the floor. He wrapped it around his waist and tucked in the corner but not before he was gifted with a whiff of her scent. Stifling the groan rising from the depths of his throat, he bit down on the inside of his cheek hard enough to draw blood. Too bad the pain did little to get his erection under control. Shit, if he didn't get it together soon, they'd both be able to go camping under the tent he was pitching.

He breathed deep in an effort to get his head on straight, but her sweet citrus scent was enough to make a grown man weep.

Alaska.

What was he going to do with the sexy girl who was so goddamn bored out of her mind that she swiped his towel for an inch, or rather eight and a half inches, of excitement?

Nothing…that's what, his last working brain cell warned.

Even though he'd spent the last six months aching to taste the girl who he'd been secretly watching over, daydreaming about ramming his cock into her so hard and fast that she'd forget what the word boredom ever meant, he knew she was off limits. He was here to protect her, and if he stepped over the line, he was as good as dead.

But Jesus, he hated seeing her so miserable, so lonely and bored that she had nothing better to do than jack his towel. If only he could give her a week of fun, break her out of this campus prison and give her the adventure she was craving. From watching her closely and tracking her every moment, he knew exactly what kind of journey this sweet yet sexy girl wanted. And damned if he didn't want to be the guy to give it to her.

Except he knew better than to blow his cover—even though he was close to blowing something—and breaking free went against all the rules.

When the hell had he become such a rule follower anyway?

CHAPTER THREE

Alaska woke to the sound of loud music blaring from her side table clock. Last night her thoughts had been preoccupied with Jesse's nakedness, but she was still pretty certain that she'd shut her alarm off. Then again, the music filling her small room proved otherwise. She stretched her limbs out and shifted on her mattress, the springs protesting with the same enthusiasm as her muscles as she rolled to her side.

With no reason to crawl out of bed early, she reached for her alarm and was about to hit the snooze button when an announcement came over the campus's radio station. She listened for a moment, then sat upright in her bed. What the hell? All she had to do to win a spring break vacation to an exclusive, invitation only resort was to answer one simple question?

Her mind raced as she reached for her IPhone. She punched in the station's number, knowing her chances of winning were good. Not only were there only a handful of students still on campus, she couldn't imagine any of them being up at this time of the morning. Hell, she wouldn't have been up either, had she remembered to shut her damn alarm off.

"Hey there," the male announcers voice came over the phone line.

Alaska's heart raced. "Hi," she said nervously.

"Who's with me today?"

"Alas...uh, it's Janey Smith."

"So Janey, all you have to do to win an all-inclusive spring break vacation is tell me, which famous Russian dancer was credited for creating the modern pointe shoe?"

Oh God, she knew this. She actually knew this!

"Anna Pavlona," she rushed out, grinning at her good fortune. Honestly, what were the odds that the question was something so near and dear to her heart?

"Congratulations," the radio guy said, then went on to say a few more things in his radio voice about a private island, things she could barely hear over the pounding of her heart.

Had she really just won?

"Your invitation and travel instructions will be here at the booth waiting for you. But there's a catch to the prize. You have to be at the booth within two hours or the trip is forfeited, so you'd better hurry."

When the line went dead, Alaska threw her legs over the side of her bed and worked to suck in air. What the hell just happened? She blinked her eyes, wondering if she was still asleep but knowing she wasn't. Had she really just won a vacation to a private island where no one knew who Alaska Rossi, or even Janey Smith, really was?

She climbed from her bed and pulled the curtains back to look out. Darkness still cloaked the campus, but the lampposts outside her widow provided sufficient illumination for her to see the snow covered grounds below. She suddenly found herself smiling, excitement clawing at her as she thought about leaving the wintry campus behind and enjoying a week of fun in the sun. But how could she go without her bodyguard trying to stop her? Surely he'd break cover to prevent her from fleeing. Then again, what were the odds that he was up? If she hurried and snuck out under the cover of darkness, he'd never know.

Moving quickly, she dropped the curtain and opened her closet to find her duffel bag. Hands shaking, she grabbed it and hastily dumped her gym and dance gear onto the floor. Once it was empty, she went to her dresser to gather her summer clothes, deciding this was the perfect opportunity to escape this concrete prison and have some much deserved fun. Heck, maybe down south she could even have an anonymous fling with a hot vacationer, or a hot local.

Or both.

Feeling a little giddy, she grabbed her bikini and beach jacket and added it to the bag. Her father would have a fit if he knew what she was doing. She could almost hear his stern words, warning that it wasn't safe for her to travel alone or to fraternize with strangers. She hesitated, fingering the zipper on the bag as a moment of common sense slipped in. Was she being too impulsive? So eager for a taste of freedom that she'd risk her safety by taking off without letting anyone know where she was going? But the invitation came from a private radio contest, right? On a campus where no one but Jesse knew who she really was? So honestly, what harm could possibly come to her on an exclusive, invitation-only island where no one knew her?

Once she had her bag packed, she tugged on her Uggs and quietly opened her door, cringing as the hinges screeched. She carefully pulled it closed behind her and tiptoed down the hall, stopping outside Jesse's door. She stood there for a moment, then pressed her ear against the wood and listened. Oddly enough, the hairs on the back of her neck began to tingle, and she got the strangest sense that he was standing on the other side of the door, listening to her as well. Fighting off the uneasy feeling and knowing it was simply her nerves at play, she hurried down the three flights of stairs leading to the main foyer and rushed outside.

The cool air whipped across her face and practically froze her lungs as she darted across the road to the building that housed the radio station. Once inside the small booth, the radio jockey, a guy she recognized from around school, asked for her ID. After she showed it, he handed her a linen envelope. She was about to ask a few questions, like who sponsored the contest and why there was such a quick turn around, but he put his head phones back on and returned to his broadcast.

Alaska turned the pretty envelope over in her hand, and her stomach fluttered when she read, "Invitation to Eden."

Oooh, it sounded so exotic and forbidden. Carefully peeling it open, she discovered Eden was a private island located somewhere in the Bermuda triangle. Naturally, she'd heard all about the 'Devil's Triangle' and the mysteries surrounding it. Some even said there was magic involved, but she didn't really believe in the supernatural and wasn't about to let anyone's superstitions stop her.

She looked over her itinerary, then checked the time on her phone. In a few short hours, a car would come to collect her and take her to the airport where she would fly to Miami. From there, she would board a boat to Eden. She stepped back outside and pulled her hood up against the bitter wind and flying snow. Feeling a moment of paranoia, she glanced around the near empty campus, half expecting to see Mr. Hotness himself leaning against the lamp pole, watching her. While she totally got off on that, she needed to lay low and figure out how to keep herself out of Jesse's crosshairs until her car arrived.

But thinking about Jesse had her gaze moving to their dorm building. She zeroed in on his bedroom window, and her breath caught. Had his curtains just moved? Surely he wasn't awake, standing at his window, watching her. Adjusting her duffle bag over her shoulder, she casually strolled toward the dance studio, positive it was just her imagination at play again but determined to cover her tracks, just in case. No way, no how was he going to blow this for her and prevent her from escaping. Unless, of course, he had a different kind of *blowing* in mind. She stole another quick glance his way, then shook some sense back into herself. Jesse couldn't be up at this ungodly hour when he didn't have to be, watching her from across the campus. Right?

* * *

Many, many hours later, Alaska found herself on a small boat, the captain taxiing her and a few other people out to Eden. As the others talked quietly amongst themselves, she stifled a yawn, gripped the brass rail on the side of the craft, and leaned over to watch the Atlantic waves splash against the vessel. A small charter plane flew overhead and caught her attention. Shading the sun from her eyes, she watched it land on a nearby island and couldn't help but think that mode of transportation would have been faster. But she was in no hurry to make her final destination, not when she could enjoy the warm breeze and salty sea spray on her face.

She reached into her bag and pulled out her invitation to take a closer look. She read the fine print to learn she'd be staying in a private cabana, overlooking the ocean. She ran her fingers over the gold embossed letters as a new sense of excitement welled up inside her.

Honestly, she had no idea what awaited her on the island, but as they approached, she glanced up in time to see a bronze plaque fixed to a rock jutting out of the water. When she read *"Welcome to Eden, where reality is whatever you wish it to be..."* her pulse leapt, and a wave of anticipation moved through her. She held her palms out, feeling a new energy in the air, a strange ripple in the wind, and suddenly, she found herself a little more anxious to arrive and a whole lot more excited to see what Eden had in store for her.

As soon as the boat docked, she disembarked and looked up to see the most lavish stone castle, its tall spires puncturing the sky. "Wow," she whispered to herself, her feet practically floating on the long wooden dock leading up to a set of magnificent marble stairs. Good God, she'd never seen anything quite so majestic and royal. It made her feel like Cinderella. Not that she believed in fairy tales. She didn't. The men in her life, who were ruled by greed and corruption, were hardly Prince Charming material.

At the top of the steps, she spotted a man scanning the arriving passengers. Dressed in black from head to toe, he had an air of command about him, but from this distance, she couldn't see his face. He shifted his stance, and he seemed to look directly at her. Her breath caught, and a strange new tingling warmed her blood.

"That is the Master of the island." She turned to see a hot Ryan Reynolds look-alike speaking to her.

"Oh," she said for lack of anything else.

"If you'll follow me," the man said as he waved his arm toward the castle. He gave her a smile that came off as both sexy and professional at the same time, a smile that told her she was about to have an unforgettable experience. "I'll get you registered and have a driver take you to your room."

Alaska lagged behind the crowd, taking in the

opulence of the island and enjoying the warmth on her skin as she walked along the dock leading to the marble stairs. She climbed the steps and walked inside the castle to discover a magnificent Greek-Roman fountain. As she examined it, the concierge came to collect her. He fitted her with a small, square sticky patch that passed as a key, assuring her it would open her room door for her, when she approached.

Dusk had fallen over Eden. Streaks of purple and pink bruised the skyline by the time she was taken to her cabana. Even though she was tired from all the travel, exhausted really, she wasn't going to let that stop her from exploring the place in search of a little excitement.

But before she set out to investigate Eden, she did a walkthrough of the cabana, loving that she had a room decorated in relaxing, beachy decor, a big, king-size bed with numerous throw pillows, and a beautiful marble bathroom with the most perfect rain shower nozzle. She grinned, knowing she was going to spend hours under the spray. She found swimming or showering the perfect way to relax after a long day.

Thrilled with her accommodations, she spread her arms, dropped her bag onto the sofa, then slid open the patio doors to enjoy the warm breeze. Beyond her wooden deck, moonlight lit up the ocean, and a nervous energy bubbled up inside her as she listened to the waves splash against the sandy shore. She stripped out of her heavy travel clothes, and foregoing panties, pulled on a light sundress. Anxious to get outside and make every single moment of this vacation count, she slipped into her flip flops.

Following the lit, tree-fringed path from her cabana, she hurried to the beach. She found it empty and decided it was the perfect opportunity to indulge in one of her naughty fantasies, skinny dipping. She was about to peel her dress from her body when she heard movement behind her. She spun, and when she spotted a man closing in on her—the same man who stood on the castle steps upon her arrival—her breath caught. The air rippled, vibrating as he approached, and the hairs on her arms stood on ends, like they'd been statically charged. Even though she was alone on a beach with a virtual stranger, she wasn't afraid. Oddly enough, there was something about him that put her at ease.

She looked into the night, and her heart lurched when she could no longer see her cabana. Not because it was obscured by palm trees or darkness, or because the lights on the path had burnt out, but because it was gone, completely and utterly missing. Everything seemed to have changed, the pink hue in the sky now an odd shade of orange, the white sand beneath her feet a golden shimmer.

What the hell?

"Welcome to Eden," the man said, his rich Greek accent eliciting a shiver from deep within her.

She looked up at the man known as the Master, but with his back to the moonlight, his face was cast in shadows.

"Thank you," she whispered, then nervously searched for her cabana again, wondering if her overtired mind was playing tricks on her. Even though she didn't believe supernatural events took place in the Bermuda triangle, she couldn't deny that something strange was going on here. It was almost like she'd tapped into an alternate reality, like her world had shifted somehow.

Welcome to Eden, where reality is whatever you wish it to be...

Pushing that ridiculous thought aside, she nibbled her bottom lip and scanned the tree line once again.

"Are you lost, Miss Smith?" he asked.

For a moment, she wondered how he knew who she was, but instead of asking, she said, "I think I might be."

She looked past his broad shoulder. "I can't seem to find my cabana."

"Perhaps that's because it's not what you're looking for."

Her back stiffened, and as she tried to puzzle out his cryptic words, he waved his hand. She followed the direction, and her breath caught when she saw a long set of stairs leading to what appeared to be an outdoor night club in the sky. She shook her head. No way was that there earlier.

"How…where…?"

"Perhaps this is what you seek."

As if pulled by an invisible force, she moved toward the stairs, the tips of her toes warming and tingling in the glittery sand. A beautiful multi-colored bird flew by, singing a melodic song as she reached the first step. With a strange sense of anticipation building up inside her, she stole a glance behind her to see if the Master was following, but just like her cabana, he had disappeared into the dark night.

She exhaled a slow breath as music drifted downward. Compelled to follow it, lured in some mysterious way, she climbed the stairs, letting the sultry beat wrap around her, seep under her skin. Her heartbeat quickened, everything inside her telling her that something promising, something forbidden, awaited her inside. When she reached the top step, she entered a circular room. Warm, overhead lighting created a soft glow over what appeared to be a high class nightclub, and when her eyes adjusted, her breath caught, a small squeaking sound rising up from her throat.

Her shock wasn't from finding a nightclub in the sky, many of its patrons wearing golden colored masks to hide their identities, nor the magnificent, three-hundred and sixty degree view of the island. No, her shock was from the scene that was taking place in the middle of the room, one that was straight out of her deepest, darkest fantasies.

Not only did the salacious sight take her by surprise, but seeing her inner most desires unfold before her eyes excited her beyond anything she'd ever known. She sucked in air as she took in the lone, chained woman standing in what appeared to be a slow-moving carousel. Except this was no child's carousel. Oh no. Not at all. This carousel was for adult play only. Instead of horses, each station had dangling chains with its own cart, a cart that held numerous play toys.

Alaska looked at the girl, who's arms were secured above her head, shackled to one of the many sets of chains dangling from the circular, overhead dome. Her long legs were spread wide for all to see while some masked man dressed only in leather pants teased and pleasured her body in the most delicious ways.

For a brief second, Alaska felt a quick flash of panic, wondering what she'd just walked in on. But when the woman moaned in bliss, her skin glistening with moisture, her head thrown back, and her mouth slack from ecstasy, Alaska felt heat bombard her body. She swallowed against the dryness in her throat, and as she perused the captive crowd, the scent of alcohol, perfume, sex, and leather curled around her.

The familiar smell of leather made her think of Jesse, made her wish he were here, experiencing all this with her. Then again, if he knew where she was and what she was doing, he'd undoubtedly drag her back home and put her on lockdown. When someone bumped her from behind, she made her way to the bar, in desperate need of alcohol.

She squeezed in between two hot guys who were enthralled by the action in the middle of the room and ordered a much needed drink. After the bartender brought her a fruity concoction, she took a long sip and spun on her stool. Heat gathered in her core as another masked guy, one who had an air of authority about him and seemed to be in charge of the club, walked from table to table, observing the patrons and their reactions. He slapped a flogger against his palm as he picked guys—who were all donning masks, which, Alaska assumed, signaled they wanted to play—and girls from the crowd.

He walked the women to the carousel, where he secured their ankles in manacles. Alaska's heart beat a little faster, her pulse quickening as she watched him restrain the girls. One girl had her clothes cut away by two well-built guys, their hands moving over her beautiful body, pinching her nipples until they grew taut. Alaska squirmed, wishing she'd worn panties, as liquid desire pooled between her thighs. She squeezed her legs together and groaned when the movement pinched her swollen clit.

The dark-haired boy on her right, who she thought was probably a college senior here for his spring break, leaned into her, the warmth of his breath wafting over her face when he asked, "What do you think? Want to play?"

"I… I…" As her words fell off, she took a huge gulp of her drink. While she loved to read all about this sort of thing, she'd never experienced anything like it in real life.

But you want to, her inner voice taunted. *You know you do*.

"That's the point," the guy with the cropped blond hair on her left said. She turned to him and took in his grin. While he was cute, he lacked the rough and tough, bad boy look Jesse had going for him. Damn. She really needed to get him out of her head. She was here to have some fun, and by fun, she meant get laid. Either one of the two guys flanking her would be perfect bedmates…or maybe even both. "You're not supposed to think. You're just supposed to feel."

"Don't worry," the dark-haired guy on her right said. "Nothing will happen if you don't want it to."

The other guy put his mouth close to her ear and said, "If you want it to stop, all you have to do is say 'Eden'."

She'd read enough BDSM books to know what he meant by that. Eden was the safe word. All she or any of the women currently tied up had to do was say the word and the play would stop. She put her straw to her lips, her mind racing, but before she could take a long pull, the masked man with the flogger stepped up to her. He opened his hand, and as he dragged the soft leather tails over his palm, her body came alive. Her flesh quivered as though the strands had actually caressed her skin, and every nerve ending tingled in anticipation.

What would those tails feel like on my backside?

His gaze met hers, and she bit back a breathy moan as the dark eyes behind the mask visually caressed her. He gave a slight nod, and there was something about him, something about his command, that told her he wasn't a man who tolerated disobedience.

"Come with me," he ordered in a tone that curled her toes.

Before Alaska even realized what she was doing, she was on her feet, blindly following him to the center of the floor to join the other women on the carousel. The masked man led her to her station, and as he secured her feet, she stood immobile, hardly able to believe what was happening. It was just this morning she was alone, feeling sorry for herself, on campus, and now she was on an exclusive island where she was about to be stripped, put on display, and pleasured in ways she'd only ever read about…*fantasized* about. Then again, it was always Biker Boy in those fantasies, not some random, masked man.

She pinched her eyes shut and opened them again, sure she was dreaming, but when she saw the crowd watching her, warm shivers of need rushed through her blood.

Holy shit.

Even though it was all happening so fast, her body burned with want, basic elemental need taking over. Some small part of her told her she should be embarrassed or frightened, but as she listened to the moans of pleasure coming from the pretty girl beside her, embarrassment was the last thing she felt. Besides, hadn't she jumped all over the campus contest because she craved to go someplace where she could lose herself, try new things, cut loose, and have some fun? Wasn't this the perfect opportunity to do just that?

"Put your hands above your head," the man said, the roughness in his voice giving way to soft persuasion as he ran one deft hand down her arm.

As his touch thrilled her, mesmerized her, she lifted her hands, and he secured her wrists to the manacles above. The sound of the chains cranking, hoisting her arms higher and higher, stretching out her body, filled her with equal amounts of fear and anticipation. Overwhelmed with what was happening, her blood pounded hard, and she remembered her safe word.

Not yet, the needy girl inside her warned. *Not yet.*

Blinking rapidly, she looked out at all the unfamiliar faces and wondered if she could really do this. The safe word lingered on her lips, but then, oddly enough, the hairs on her nape tingled, and she felt like she was being watched, not by the anonymous crowed, but by the one and only guy she wanted watching her. She gave a broken gasp and searched through the sea of masked men, searching for Jesse, but her thoughts fragmented when someone stepped up behind her.

She sucked in a tight breath when she felt the leather

tails trailing down her body and gave a cry of pain and pleasure when they came down across her ass. Even though she still had her sundress on, the tails stung her sensitive cheeks just the same. A second man stepped up to her, and she could feel her dress being cut away, exposing her naked body beneath.

When the second hit came on her bare backside, she closed her eyes, imagining it was Jesse watching her, spanking her, touching her aching body. It filled her with want, and she moved her hips, flustered, anxious...so damn needy for the man who would never treat her as anything more than a mobster's daughter under his care.

Chapter Four

Jesse stood back from the crowd and watched Alaska, watched the way her beautiful, pale nipples tightened with arousal each time the flogger hit her ass, the way the overhead light glistened on her pretty pink pussy as it moistened with need.

His mouth watered, and he drew in a harsh breath in an effort to bank the want riding through his veins. As he let the air hiss out slowly, he drove his hands into his pockets and rocked on his feet. Just because Alaska was hands off to him didn't mean he couldn't give her what she wanted. And if there was one guy who knew what Alaska wanted, it was him, considering he'd been studying her every move for months.

His mind drifted back to the night he caught her masturbating, and he shifted his stance, adjusting his thickening cock. Fuck, it had taken all his restraint not to strip off his clothes and join her in the shower, because not only did she get to him in a way no other girl ever had before, there was something so sexy, so honest and open about her when she lost herself like that.

The truth was, he knew everything about her, from

how she spent her days, and more importantly, how she spent her nights…including the kinds of books she read and the way she danced like her life depended on it. Her actions told him so much about her, about what she liked…*needed.*

Not that she could ever act on her needs, or actually go after what she wanted. Alaska had spent her whole life powerless, stifled under a domineering man who controlled her every move. But here on Eden, the power was all hers. She might be the one restrained on that carousel, but when it came right down to it, *she* was the one calling the shots. And that was exactly what she needed.

Christ, he hated the way her father treated her, the way he so easily dismissed her like she was nothing but an annoying piece of lint on his coat. Even though Franco had never laid a hand on her, to Jesse, abuse was abuse, physical or emotional. Maybe that's why he volunteered for this assignment. He had a sense of protectiveness in him, which undoubtedly stemmed from his own fucked up childhood.

His fingers went to the tattoo scroll on his arm, one that hid years of abuse. His gut clenched as he thought about his older sister and how powerless he was to protect her from their bastard father. The prick had taken turns beating the shit out of them. At the time, he'd been too young to stop it, but he swore he'd never see another girl suffer at the hands of a man, especially her father. As long as he was around, no one was ever going to hurt Alaska. The truth was he cared about her, which is why he wanted to give her the escape, the attention, she was craving.

He refocused his thoughts and watched her from across the room, gauging her reactions as the man behind the mask pleasured her. Instead of waiting for the carousel to circle back his way, Jesse followed it, keeping a wide berth. He pulled in a fortifying breath, his mind shifting through all the things he wanted to do to her himself, if only she wasn't off limits.

For a brief second, her glance met his and his heart lurched. But when her dark eyes glazed over with lust, he knew she hadn't made the connection. His job was to keep a level of separation and his true identity a secret, which meant that he couldn't let her know it was him who'd arranged this, going to great measure to ensure she thought she'd won a contest and making sure she was safe while she indulged in her fantasies.

Jesse had known about this secret island for a long time, and between him and the guards patrolling the nightclub, as well as the shoreline, he knew she'd be safe here. Years ago, before Franco Rossi plucked his scarred and battered body off the streets and gave a him job, he used to street fight for cash. After one particularly bad brawl, while he was in the back room getting bandaged, he overheard two rich business men, men who'd just won thousands of dollars off Jesse's fight, discuss a place called Eden—a place where fantasies came true.

At that point in his life, Eden sounded like heaven. But with what little money he made back then, Eden was out of his reach. It still wasn't within his means, but he'd called in a few favors to bring Alaska here, to give her this brief taste of freedom.

Even though he'd never stepped foot on the island before, after learning more about it, he knew it was the perfect place for Alaska to blow off some steam before classes resumed after the break. From the books she read, he knew what kind of sexual playground he'd walk into tonight, considering it was a combination of her inner most fantasy and the island's magic.

Perhaps after a week of living out her darkest fantasies, Alaska would go home happy, sexually sated. Then maybe she'd stop teasing the fuck out of him.

When it came to her, sooner or later, his armor was going to crack. Once that happened, there wasn't a man alive who could stop him from stepping over that invisible, forbidden line. The line he knew better than to cross, for both their sakes.

The masked man touched her, sliding his hands all over her lithe body. The urgency and emotion on her face had his dick aching. Damned if he didn't want to be the one fulfilling her needs. The other women on the carousel moaned with ecstasy, but Jesse's attention was on Alaska. The man in control of her pleasure pulled a small pink vibrator off the tray behind him and switched it on.

Alaska's eyes grew wide, her mouth opened, and for a moment, Jesse wondered if she was going to use her safe word. But the second the man slid the toy between her spread legs, her head lolled to the side, and she clamped her mouth shut.

Jesus, she was so fucking sexy. His cock ached, his balls tightening as a tremor moved through him and a storm brewed inside his body. He cursed and fought the natural inclination to go to her. Claim her.

The man teased her pussy with the vibrator, and she rolled her hips forward, her body conveying what she needed. Her lashes fluttered shut, and she caught her lip between her teeth. Jesse growled, loving that look on her face, one he desperately wanted to put there. Sweat trickled down his forehead, and blood pounded through his veins as he watched her climax build, her throaty purr practically resonating through his body when it finally overtook her.

When she stopped moaning and hung limp in the chains, he watched her carefully. Sated and exhausted, and no doubt drowning in a sea of emotions and sensations, her chest rose and fell erratically. The man controlling the scene stepped up to her. He touched her forehead, and her heavy-lidded eyes closed. When her body sagged, her knees giving out, it prompted Jesse into action.

With his mask firmly in place and knowing he was in charge of her after care, he hurried forward and gestured for the carousel to stop. When it came to a smooth halt, he stepped up to her and pitched his voice low to disguise it. "I've got you," he whispered.

She let loose a soft, mewling sound as he unleashed her hands and ankles. He gathered her into his arms and smiled down at her as she worked to keep her eyes open. The long day of travel, combined with the emotionally and physically draining scene she'd just played a part in, had zapped the last vestige of her energy. Jesse grabbed her dress, accepted the blanket that was handed to him, and wrapped her in it. The sweet scent of her skin thickened his cock as he carried her from the club and down the long stretch of stairs to the beach below. He walked to her cabana and the door opened as he approached. He deposited her on the bed, pulled her blankets over her, and set her dress on the chair beside him. As she snuggled in, he fought an internal battle to wake her, climb between the sheets with her, and fuck her until the wee hours of the morning.

Instead, he watched her until she fell into a deep sleep, loving the way her hair fell in soft curls across the pillow, the way her full lips opened slightly, her soft breathing sounds cutting through the quiet. Once he was sure she was safe and no longer in need of his care, he slipped from her cabana and made his way back to his, intent on taking a hot shower and abusing the hell out of his aching cock.

* * *

Alaska awoke to the sounds of a bird chirping outside

her window. Where the hell was she? She peeled her eyes open, unease tightening her gut as she examined the unfamiliar surroundings. She blinked, then rubbed the sleep from her eyes in an effort to orient herself. Suddenly, the memories of the previous night came rushing back in a whoosh, and she sat up, darting a glance around her room. She swallowed against the dryness in her throat, her mind racing as fragments of the night before began to fall into place.

Had last night been a dream? Had she actually done those things?

A sound crawled out of her throat as she tossed her blankets off to find herself naked. She remembered her dress being cut away but couldn't recall going back to her cabana, or going to bed. She'd had one drink…had someone slipped something in it?

She searched through the recesses of her mind, vaguely remember being carried, vaguely remembering the warm scent of leather. It reminded her of Jesse, but she knew he couldn't be here. She looked at her body. There were no welts on her skin, which meant the masked man was either very skilled with a whip or last night had never happened at all. She shifted, and the muscles in her arms hurt, like they'd been stretched. When she saw the rub marks on her wrists and the dress on her chair, she knew it couldn't have been a dream.

A warm shiver moved through her, and moisture pooled between her legs. Good God, had she really let some man tie her up while another pleasured her in front of a crowd?

You did and you loved it, the vixen inside her whispered.

Pushing her hair off her face, she rushed to the shower, desperate to get outside to see if the nightclub in the sky really did exist. She washed quickly, and after dressing in a pair of shorts and a t-shirt, sandals in hand,

Alaska walked the tree-fringed path back to the beach. She stood near the water and shaded the sun from her eyes as she scanned the area, but for the life of her, she couldn't find the night club. Even though it sounded ridiculous, she couldn't help but wonder if it was only visible at night, some trick of the island or the moonlight.

Some trick of the mind...

She turned and looked up and down the beach. Padded lounge chairs shaded by grass umbrellas dotted the sandy shore. At the far end of the beach, she spotted a Tiki bar with a bartender mixing drinks under the straw roof. A crowd gathered, laughing as they enjoyed early morning cocktails. She walked toward the hut, her heart beating a little faster as she took in the naked sunbathers dotting the shoreline.

She continued along the long stretch of sand, her feet in the water as the puzzle of the mysterious nightclub continued to plague her. Off in the distance, boats bobbed in the sea, and as she examined them, that old familiar feeling of being watched washed over her. She licked her dry lips and looked around, but when her glance came up empty, she fought down the unease, missing Jesse's constant presence. With all these strange things going on, maybe she should have let someone know where she was going.

She made her way to the paved path and came upon a large map that detailed the island. She found the 'you are here' star and ran her finger along the trail leading to the castle. After getting lost on the winding turns despite the map, she took the corner and finally found a huge outdoor pavilion. Walking through the crowd, many of who were lounging on wicker furniture, checking emails or enjoying an early morning drink at the bar, she looked for a familiar face, someone who might have been at the club last night and could fill her on what was going on.

Delicious smells reached her nostrils as she moved around the furniture, and when she heard music, she followed the sound. She walked until she came to a huge stage and found dancers, out of costume, practicing for a show. Quietly watching them for a while, admiring and committing their choreographed moves to memory, she lowered herself into one of the chairs. Her body swayed as she continued to study their moves, everything inside her longing to go up there, to be a part of the show.

One of the male dancers caught her eyes, and she felt herself blush when he gave her a sexy wink. Had he been one of the masked men last night?

A middle-aged man came onto stage, clearly the director. He clapped his hands and gave direction, then he looked at Alaska. He planted his palms on his hips and asked, "Are you just going to sit there?"

Alaska sat up straighter. Surely to God, he couldn't be talking to her.

"I...what?" she asked.

"Are you just going to sit there or are you going to dance?"

"I'm not one of the dancers," she said.

He folded his arms, his busy brow furrowing. "Then what are you doing here?"

"I was just watching."

"The show isn't until tonight, honey. Come back then." He turned his back to her.

After being dismissed and wishing she really was one of the dancers—after all, performing on a stage like that would be a dream come true for her—she retraced her steps. But instead of finding herself back at the pavilion, she walked into a beautiful outdoor, breakfast area. She was instantly greeted by a hot guy who led her to a private table with a spectacular view of the ocean. Even though she was used to being alone, a strange sense of loneliness came over her as she sat by herself, missing

Jesse's distant yet constant presence. The empty chairs beside her a sad reminder that she had no one to enjoy the view with. Was she just destined to be alone? Would everyone in her life eventually abandon her?

When a waiter came with coffee, she redirected her thoughts, refusing to dwell on anything but this vacation, even though there seemed to be strange things going on. She blew into her cup then took a sip, hoping that after breakfast, she could find the two guys she sat between at the bar last night. As if thinking about them had conjured them up, they sauntered up to her.

"Mind if we join you?"

She blinked up at them and took in their mischievous smiles. "Sure," she answered and resisted the urge to pinch them to make sure they were real. Instead, she fiddled with her cup as they sat, flanking her once again.

The one with the dark hair and even darker eyes jabbed his thumb into his chest, and oh what a fine chest it was. "I'm Jack," he said, then nodded toward his friend, "and he's Blair."

Alaska swallowed a mouthful of coffee and turned to Blair. He flashed a bright smile and ran his hands through his cropped blond hair. She took in his features, then let her glance dropped to his shoulders. As she admired his well-built body, her skin flushed hot.

With the air around them charging, sexual energy zinging between them all, she set her cup down and tried for casual. "I'm Janey," she said. The waiter came with more coffee, and they went quiet as he filled their cups. As soon as he left, Alaska leaned into Jack, deciding to get right to the point. "Last night," she began, wondering how she could ask about the mysterious club without sounding like she was certifiable. "The night club—"

"Yeah, thanks for that," Jack said, his sexy grin widening.

Her brow furrowed, and she straightened in her seat.

"What do you mean?"

"It was a great scene," Blair said, tapping his temple. "I like the way you think."

What the hell? They were acting like it was she who'd arranged the scene.

"I..." she began again. "I went looking for the club this morning, and...um...it wasn't there." When both men looked at her like she was dense, she fidgeted nervously in her chair. "What?" she asked.

From her peripheral vision, she spotted the Master walking through the breakfast area. Even though she still couldn't make out his face, she knew it was him by the dark suit and the way he carried himself. She was about to jump up, to demand answers—after all, he was the one who'd pointed the club out to her—when Jack's hand came down on her shoulder. His dark eyes narrowed when he asked, "You do know what this place is, right?"

"Eden," she answered, thinking about the invitation. "A vacation island."

"Yes, but it's more than that."

"More than that?" she asked nervously.

"Jesus, you really don't know, do you?"

"Know what?"

"Who gave you the invitation?" Blair asked.

"I won it. It was on a campus radio contest."

The two guys exchanged a look, and her head bobbed back and forth, trying to figure out what it was she was missing.

What do they know that I don't?

Jack leaned back in his chair, his leg brushing hers under the table. "It's a place where reality is whatever you wish it to be. Surely you were told that."

She lowered her voice, and her breath came shallow when she said, "I don't understand."

Blair nudged closer. "Last night happened because

it's what you wanted to happen, Janey." He put his hand over hers, and warmth surged through her veins. "The scene was from your fantasies."

She gulped and shook her head as her body tightened with erotic memories. "No way." If the scene was from her imagination, then she had no doubt that Jesse would have taken the starring role. "I didn't even know those men."

"You pick the scene, not the cast," Jack said.

Okay, so there was no denying that she'd fantasized about being tied up and pleasured, but last night's scene was way over the top—beyond even *her* wildest imagination. "You guys are just messing with me."

Blair arched a brow, and his thick muscles shifted as he moved even closer, the warm scent of his skin washing over her. "What's strange is that this wasn't explained to you. The person who extended the invitation should have laid out the details."

"I told you. I won it."

Once again, the two guys exchanged a confused look.

Her fingers tightened around her mug, and she went silent for a moment as she cast her eyes down in thought, trying to wrap her brain around what they were saying. "I still don't believe any of this," she murmured.

"No?" Jack's voice was rich, darkly seductive, when he said, "Then join us at dusk."

Her stomach tightened with a mixture of apprehension and intrigue as she met his eyes. "What happens at dusk?"

"That's up to you."

"Meet us at the dock and bring your bathing suit," Blair said. "We'll catch the party boat and go on an adventure."

"Party boat?" she asked, a shiver skipping down her spine. "What kind of adventure?"

Blair's grin widened, the promise in his voice

undeniable when he answered with, "Whatever kind you want."

45

Chapter Five

With Blair's parting words rattling around inside her brain, Alaska spent the rest of the day touring the beautiful island. She walked through the majestic castle and browsed the spa and boutiques before she took a trolley ride around the outskirts of Eden. As she kept one eye out for the Master, she spoke with several guests over the afternoon, but since none had mentioned anything about this island fulfilling fantasies, or altering realties, she didn't bring it up, either. Partly because she was still convinced that Jack and Blair were messing with her and partly because if what had happened last night was due to the mystery and mystique of The Triangle, and they weren't yanking her chain, she didn't want to blow a good thing. She had a lot of fantasies saved up, and this was an opportunity too good to pass.

The sun dipped beneath the horizon, turning the sky a pretty shade of pink as Alaska walked the beach. She grabbed a fruity drink from the guy working the Tiki bar and sipped on it as she splashed in the warm Atlantic surf. Breathing in the fresh, salty air, she exhaled slowly, watching the boats bobbing in the distance. She tipped her wrist and checked the time. Equal amounts of anticipation and nervousness invaded her stomach as she thought about making her way to the dock and boarding a boat where *anything she wanted to happen,* would happen.

With her sandals dangling from her finger tips, she spun on her toes and made her way back to her cabana, but as she entered the palm-fringed path, the sound of a motorcycle revving reached he ears.

Jesse…

She ran the length of the path, rushing past her cabana, and when she found herself on one of the many winding roads, she glanced left then right, searching for the source of the sound. A jeep carrying two passengers in the backseat slowed as it reached her.

"Need a lift?" the dark-skinned driver asked.

She shook her head, was about to leave, then blurted out, "Wait, did you see a motorcycle go by?"

"No ma'am," he said.

She frowned, and thinking she was losing it, looked up and down the road one last time and said, "Okay, thanks."

"Were you interested in riding one?" he asked.

"So you do have bikes available for guest to use?"

His grin widened. "This is Eden," he stated simply, a twinkle in his eye. "We have everything you need."

After he left, she continued on to her cabana, reliving the conversation she'd had with Jack and Blair. Wanting to figure out if they were right, if this place really was about fulfilling her fantasies, she hurried to her cabana and went straight to the shower to wash the sand from her skin. She turned on the hot spray and gave herself a good hard lecture. She'd come here to cut loose and currently had two hot guys expecting her on the party boat, so it was well past time to put Jesse out of her thoughts and go for it. It wasn't like he wanted her or cared about her in any way. Sure, he watched out for her, but only because he was being paid to do so.

With renewed purpose, she finished washing, taking extra time on her hair and makeup, then grabbed her bikini from her bag. She pulled it on and spun in the mirror, noting that the fit was tighter than last year. Her hips had grown a little curvier, her breasts a little fuller, the triangle patches barely covering her pale areolas. She took her breasts into her hands and enjoyed the heavy feel of them in her palms. Since it was the only suit she had with her, and she had very little cash to buy a new one at the boutique she'd visited this morning, it would have to do. She didn't dare use her credit card as her father would get the bill and find out she had snuck off to the island for a little R&R.

Gathering her bravado, she shimmied into a short skirt, tugged on a snug t-shirt, and went to the path to wave down a jeep. Darkness blanketed the night as the driver dropped her off. She walked the wooden dock, the multi-colored bird she'd spotted last night flying by as she listened to laughter coming from the boat. Although it wasn't really a boat, it was more like a giant, triple-deck party barge.

She was greeted by a young guy who held her hand as she stepped on. Once on board, she glanced through the sea of people laughing, drinking, and twerking to the loud music. She smiled and wondered if this was being filmed for 'Girls Gone Wild."

Making a beeline to the bar, she grabbed a stool and ordered a drink. The bartender handed her a coconut with a straw. She took a long sip, and when her mouth exploded with the delicious flavor of coconut and rum, she moaned in bliss.

"It's good, huh?"

She spun around to find Jack standing over her, a sexy grin on his face as his dark eyes moved to her snug t-shirt, specifically, her protruding nipples. She held the drink out to him. "Try it."

He put his mouth around the straw and took a taste. When he pulled back and licked his lips, a strange tingling raced through her blood, warming her from the inside out. "Yeah, it's good," he murmured, then leaned into her, the beachy scent of his skin washing over her. "How about another taste?"

She lifted the coconut again, but he put his hand over hers to stop her and instead, pressed his lips to hers. Caught off guard by his boldness, she gave a little whimper, but then she reminded herself she was here to have fun, to let whatever was going to happen...happen. When she didn't push him off and instead leaned into him, he cupped her head and held her to him. His mouth was gentle at first, but when she opened for him, enjoying the flavor of his lips, his tongue moved inside to play with hers.

He inched back and said, "Tastes even better." Before she could catch her breath, he grabbed her hand and lifted her from the stool. "Come on."

"Where?"

"Top deck. The view is amazing."

He guided her through the throng of partygoers, and she admired his broad, naked back, the muscles tightening and relaxing again as she followed him up the stairs. Once they reached the very top level, he pulled her against him, his hands going to the sensitive area at the small of her back. Alaska sucked in a breath when she spotted an elevated stage. The same guy she'd watched dance during rehearsal earlier that day—the one who'd given her a sexy wink—along with a pretty blonde girl, mimicked sex as they moved together in perfect synch. She couldn't help but stare at him. With a lean, muscular body and dressed in nothing but a pair of spandex shorts that showcased the hard ridge of his cock, the guy had a body to die for. Then again, so did the sexy girl he was with.

She shot Jack a sidelong glance. "So I take it this the view you were talking about?"

Jacks grin grew wicked. "Oh yeah. Come here," he commanded, his voice dripping with promise. He grabbed her by the waist, pulled her against him, and pushed through the crowd until they were closer to the stage. A shudder moved through her as she watched the dancers, and she could feel her heart race a little faster, the hungry spot between her legs growing a little wetter, a little needier.

The barge pulled away from the dock, moving them deeper into the Atlantic waters. She rocked against Jack, and his hands tightened on her body. His fingers burned over her flesh, and when she looked up at him, he shot her a smoldering look.

She felt another body press up against her and turned her head to see Blair. He pushed his hard cock against her ass, and a moan lodged in her throat. Okay, so there was no denying that she'd fantasized about having two men, but the truth was she'd never envisioned a scene quite like this before.

Still skeptical and thinking the two were toying with her, she began, "Jack?"

"Yeah," he asked, his voice huskier than it was moments ago.

"How can you say this is from my imagination, my fantasy, when I've never even been on a boat like this before and never even knew what one looked like?"

Instead of answering, he smiled and cupped her chin to aim her glance toward the stage. She turned in time to see the pretty girl jump into the crowd, the hot male dancer looking directly at her. When he crooked his finger, her breath caught.

"Go on up there, baby," Jack whispered into her ear.

"Go perform for us."

"You know you want to," Blair added, his hands tracing her curves in promising ways.

They gave her a nudge, and a shiver skipped down her spine as a path seemed to clear for her. Even though she considered herself a dancer and had taken many lessons, she'd never *dirty* danced in front of a crowd before. A laugh bubbled up in her throat, because after last night, how could she be nervous about a little sexy dancing when some masked man had tied her up and pleasured her?

The dancer's strong hand reached out to her, and when she put her palm in his, he hoisted her up. Her body crashed against his, and he dipped his head, his mouth close to hers. "What's your name, sweetness?"

"It's Janey," she answered. With her thoughts so rattled, she couldn't believe she remembered to use her alias.

"I'm Caleb," he said as he spun her around until her back was pressed against his chest. He put his mouth close to her ear and whispered, "Follow my lead, sweetheart."

A slow burn worked its way through her body as he ran his hands down her arms, lifting them over his head. She moved against him, her hips rocking as she followed the sway of his body. Every movement sensual, he trailed his fingers back down her raised arms, sweeping the outer edge of her breasts, until he gripped the hem of her short skirt. Grabbing a fistful in his hands, he lifted it slightly and touched her inner thighs. The crowd cheered, and when she searched for a familiar face and found Jack and Blair's eyes on her, it made her feel sexy, desirable.

Wanted.

She wet her mouth, and when Jack grinned at her antics, it urged her on. The music blared, and they both rocked against each other like they'd practiced the routine long before tonight. But tonight wasn't about rehearsed dance moves, it was about instinct and letting hers guide the way. She briefly closed her eyes, allowing herself to get lost in Caleb's touch, his body, his sexy movements.

A tremble moved through her. God, there was no denying that she loved to dance, perform...be watched. It was only six months ago that she realized she had such exhibitionist tendencies. It was so crazy, so wild, so delightfully scandalous.

Caleb's mouth moved to her neck, and heat bombarded her when he lightly ran his lips over the long column of her throat. With her thighs trembling, lust rose to the surface as he stimulated her senses. Her body buzzed to life, little jolts of electricity firing her synapses as moisture pooled between her quivering thighs. She lowered her hands and cupped her breasts, rubbing her thumbs over her hard nipples. Once again, cheers erupted, but she couldn't think about that, not when Caleb was dipping under her skirt, running his fingers along the seam of her bikini bottoms.

With his mouth hot against her skin and his cock hard against her back, she found herself relaxing into him, wondering if he was going to fuck her right here on stage with everyone watching. She quivered, the thoughts of being watched, being wanted, thrilling her. But there was another part of her, one that wanted only one man to desire her.

He dipped a finger inside her bikini bottoms and swiped the rough pad of his thumb over her clit. Oh, God. Her head fell back against him, and she jerked her hips forward, demanding more.

Her body flared hot, and her lashes fluttered against the flood of heat, but when she heard Jack's voice over the others, cheering her on, her lids opened.

Caleb pushed a finger inside her, and she cried out, need urging her on. Jesus, she wanted this, wanted to come up here on stage with everyone watching. Her body was screaming for release, and she was so close, but she wanted more…she wanted… God, she didn't know what she wanted.

With her brain going a mile a minute, Jack stepped up to the stage and reached a hand out for her. Panting wildly, her body still trembling, so close to letting go, she stood there, staring at him, barely able to comprehend what he was doing.

"Looks like you have something else in mind for tonight," Caleb said. He put his mouth near her ear and whispered, "You're a natural performer. Come find me at rehearsal sometime this week."

"What? Why?" she asked, her body so revved up she could barely think straight.

"The dance troupe needs someone like you."

She was about to tell him she was only here for a week, but her words were lost on a moan when Blair stepped up beside Jack and gripped her by the waist to lift her off the stage. He drew her to him, and she slid down his body, his huge erection pressing into her. When her feet finally touched the floor, he brushed her hair from her forehead and said, "You're burning up, baby."

"I know just what she needs," Jack announced, reaching for her hand. He gave a little tug and led her down two sets of stairs to the main deck. Sandwiched between the two guys, she followed along until Jack stopped on what appeared to be a tanning station with a small board for diving.

"Let's go for a swim," he said.

She hesitated and looked into the dark ocean. A tremble moved through her, and she couldn't help but feel a little afraid to dive in at night.

"Don't worry, baby," Jack said. "We won't let anything happen to you."

Oddly enough, she knew he was right, knew that here on Eden, a place that had an aura of mystery about it, she felt completely safe.

"Let us take you where you need to go," Blair said, the blatant invitation in his voice bringing her attention back to him. "Besides, we're not going far." He pointed to a wharf bobbing in the near distance, numerous boats in the vicinity. She quivered at the thought of swimming out there, finding herself alone and on display as these two men pleasured her.

"Last one there is a rotten egg," Jack teased.

Before she could stop herself, her favorite childhood response to that silly saying spilled from her lips. "The first one has to eat it."

"Deal," the guys said in unison before jumping in.

"Hey," she blurted out before stripping off her clothes and diving in after them.

The water felt gloriously cool against her fevered skin, but did little to quell the heat between her legs. She swam underwater then rose, inches from the dock. She looked up to see Jack and Blair standing over her. Caleb was right. She did have something else in mind for tonight. They reached down, each gripping an arm to pull her from the water.

As they positioned her between them, and her breath rushed from her lungs, a bevy of fantasies flitted through her mind. While she'd never been with two men before, especially two this hot, there was a part of her that wanted to try this.

Jack ran his thumb over her mouth. "I've wanted to fuck you since that first night at the club," he murmured, his eyes so dark, so full of heat, her nipples tightened almost painfully.

"And I've been dying to taste you," Blair said from

behind her, his hands all over her body.

"Now what was this about eating…?" Jack questioned, a teasing edge to his voice as his fingers slipped between her legs.

She opened her mouth to tell him it was just a silly saying when his lips crashed down on hers, stealing her response. He kissed her hard, and from behind, Blair pulled her hair from her shoulders. "How about I go first," he whispered.

Tension rose in her as he kissed a path down her neck, untying her bikini top along the way. Once he released the strings, it fell to the ground, and Jack groaned as her breasts pressed up against his naked chest. He broke the kiss and dipped his head, closing one hot mouth over her hard nipple. She arched into him, loving the feel of her breasts encased in his warm hands as Blair sank to his knees behind her. Deft fingers gripped the band on her bikini bottom, and she wiggled slightly as he shimmied it down her legs. He reached her feet and tapped her inner thigh. Reading his silent command, she lifted one foot then the other, kicking the wet scrap of material aside.

After a good hard suck on one nipple, Jack spun her around. He held her tight against him as she faced Blair. "Open for him," Jack demanded in a soft tone. "Show him your pussy."

With Blair still on his knees, she widened her legs, and his nostrils flared as he reached out to pull her wet lips open. He spent a long time just looking at her, and she could feel herself grow wetter.

"So fucking pretty," he murmured before he leaned in to swipe his tongue over her clit.

"Oh, God," she whispered with effort. As her knees weakened, Jack held her tighter, his hands once again going to her breasts as he packaged her against him. Blair gripped her thighs and buried his face between her legs, his tongue circling her swollen clit before plunging hungrily. His hair tickled her inner thighs while the soft blade of his tongue did the most delicious things to her pussy. She moaned without censor as the fresh sea breeze whipped over her hot body, doing little to cool it down. One thick finger pushed inside her, and her body responded with a shudder.

Jack continued to pinch her nipples, the erotic sensation traveling to her inner core. She could hear cheers coming from a boat as it passed, and it gave her a secret thrill to know she was being watched.

"You like that, baby?" Jack asked, pinching her nipples harder.

Since a reply was beyond her, she whimpered and concentrated on the points of pleasure between her legs as Blair feasted on her. A second finger joined the first, and her body went up in a burst of flames.

Feeling wild, reckless, delirious with pleasure, she rocked her hips, rubbing herself against Blair's mouth as he finger fucked her. She began to shake, the tension in her body escalating, then, in a haze of arousal, an explosion tore through her, her muscles clenching hard around Blair's fingers. Her knees gave out, and if Jack hadn't been holding her, she would have collapsed in a heap.

"That's it, baby," Jack said, as Blair continued to lick her, soothing her sex as she rode out the last waves of her orgasm. "Take what you need."

When the scent of her arousal reached his nostrils, Jack groaned and rubbed his cock against her back. "I need to fuck you. Now."

He pulled a foil packet out of his pocket, kicked off his shorts, and sheathed himself as Blair stretched out on the wharf and pulled her on top of him. He kissed her hard, and she could taste herself on his mouth. Before she could even catch her breath, Jack grabbed her hips and flipped her over. From below her, Blair captured her legs in his and spread them wide, completely exposing her to anyone interested in looking.

Jack gazed at her naked body and trailed his fingers over her breasts, her stomach, stopping when he reached her pussy. He stroked her, then slipped a finger inside.

"Are you ready for me?" he asked.

She nodded as he climbed up her body, his crown breaching her opening. His skimmed his mouth over her breasts, his weight coming down on her and Blair. As their three bodies melded together, Jack jerked his hips forward, driving the length of him into her.

She opened her mouth, but he swallowed her cry with a kiss. He slammed deep, his teeth scraping her lower lip as he chased an orgasm. Gripping her shoulders, he angled his body to pound hard, and Blair groaned into her ear as he slid his hands around her waist to play with her nipples.

Jack continued to fuck her, long, hard strokes that sent her higher and higher. Her nails bit into his shoulder, and she whimpered as her passion soared. She gave a breathy cry as Jack's body began to tense, his muscles bunching. Knowing he was only a stroke away, she gave herself over to the pleasure. Her throat clenched, and her body convulsed as her pussy muscles tightened and contracted around his throbbing cock. Jack threw his head back, stilled, and joined her in orgasm.

His breathing labored, Jack depleted himself inside her then collapsed on top of her, burying his face in her neck as they both recovered from their climax. She touched his back, running her fingers over his moist skin, his rigid muscles relaxing beneath her soothing touch.

As she lay trapped between these two awesome guys, her passion receding, a strange, uneasy feeling moved into her stomach. Her hands stilled on Jack's back, and her brain took that moment to think about the lump pushing into her throat.

The sex was good. Really good. These two were skilled and definitely knew their way around a woman's body. So why then did she suddenly feel so lost, so completely empty inside?

Because it was lacking intimacy, a real connection, her inner voice warned.

She'd come here to have fun and get laid. But as she found herself sandwiched between these hot guys, it occurred to her that she still felt lonely. That sobering reality startled her and had her questioning what it would take to fulfill her, to make her feel loved…important.

A noise in the distance caught her attention. She lifted her head, and when the hairs on her nape began to tingle, her breathing became shallow.

She peered into the night and caught the silhouette of a guy standing on the upper deck of a boat. Her heart jumped into her throat, and her body tightened. There was something about him that held her attention, something about the way he stood there with tension in his posture, tracking her every movement, that felt oh so familiar.

Jack lifted his head, worried eyes moving over her face, when he asked, "Hey baby, are you okay?"

"He's here," she murmured, her voice a strangled whisper. "I just know it."

Blair ran soothing fingers down her arm and in a soft tone asked, "Who's here, sweetheart?"

"Jesse."

CHAPTER SIX

After waking up early, Alaska dressed in a simple, button down sundress, slipped into her flip flops, and hurried outside. She spent the better part of the day searching the island for Jesse, trying to catch a glimpse of him in the crowd. She checked with registration, but they had no record of a Jesse Cavanaugh ever arriving on Eden. Then again, he could be using an alias like her. As day bled to night, she paced the beach, searching endlessly for signs of him. Everything in her gut told her he was here, watching her.

Feeling frustrated, she began the trek back to her room, squishing the warm sand between her toes. She slipped on her flip flops when she reached the lit path leading to her cabana, but when she heard a motorcycle revving in the distance, she stilled her movements and listened carefully. She caught the sound again and parted a few tree branches to peer into the woods. The beautiful multi-colored bird that seemed to be following her spread its wings and took flight, startling her. With her pulse pounding, she pushed tree branches out of her way, determined to find Jesse and figure out what was going on.

The trees grew thicker, the canopy of leaves over her head blocking out the moonlight and making it difficult to find her way out. Something moved in the underbrush, and feeling a little nervous, she hurried forward, fearing she was never going to find her way out, or worse, find a snake slithering underfoot. A few feet later, the trees thinned and she stepped from the wooded area. She glanced at the huge clubhouse overlooking the ocean, numerous motorcycles parked outside. It occurred to her that the trolley tour she'd taken the day after she arrived had never passed through this area, or if it had, the building wasn't there at the time. As she examined the clubhouse, she wondered whether this was another fantasy, or if she'd just stumbled upon Jesse.

Her pulse leapt, and with renewed purpose, she hurried toward the building. She could hear music from the open windows as she looked over all the motorcycles, searching for one that Jesse might drive. Pushing her mussed hair from her face in an attempt to fix herself up after her trek through the woods, she opened the door, giving her eyes a moment to adjust.

The sound of balls cracking on a pool table pulled her focus, and she looked at the men walking the table and drinking beer, oblivious to her. She scanned their faces and catalogued the room but was forced to step out of the way when three men came barreling in behind her, all wearing leather beanie caps, with bandanas masking their faces. A fine shiver moved through her as she studied the skull pattern on their masks. She looked at their gang colors and the patches on their leather jackets, patches that identified them as…outlaws.

As the three men made a commotion, their biker boots hitting the wooden floor hard as they kicked off debris, all eyes in the club turned her way. Her stomach tightened. Feeling like she'd just walked into the lion's den, she took a step back, hoping to lose herself in the shadows.

Too bad the guy who appeared to be the gang's leader seemed to have other plans.

"Well, well… What do we have here?" he asked, stepping away from the pool table. He walked around her, and she could feel his eyes sizing her up. Everything in the way he moved told her he was the one in charge, the alpha.

He stopped in front of her, and she lifted her gaze. Her heart leapt when she came face-to-face with a guy who could easily double as Charlie Hunnam, the sexy actor who played Jackson from Sons of Anarchy.

Oh Gawd…

He cupped her chin, and as he turned her face from left to right, giving her a thorough examination, it occurred to her that this man—this scene—was straight from her fantasies.

He grinned. "Looks like we found ourselves a trespasser," he said.

"I didn't…" she began. "I'm looking for… I'm not looking for trouble."

He pressed his finger to her lips to silence her. "Yeah, well I think you just found it," he responded, his voice dropping an octave. He took a step closer, his hard body crowding hers. He dipped his head, and she could smell beer on his breath, leather on his skin. His mouth was so close to hers she thought he was going to kiss her. "You're trespassing, sweet thing, and you do know what we do with trespassers around these parts, right?" he asked, his strong hands going to her hips.

"Hell, yeah," a few of the guys hollered out. Chairs scraped across the floor as the men rose, preparing for what, she had no idea.

"No, what?" she asked, her voice a low strained

whisper as she worked to figure out how this fantasy was going to play out. She wasn't even sure she wanted it to, not if Jesse wasn't involved.

Promise dripped from his voice when he said, "We punish them."

"Punish?" she squeaked out, her mind conjuring up the kind of punishment this dangerous biker dude could dole out.

He stepped behind her, his fingers tightening on her waist. He pressed his chest to her back, and with a little nudge, set her in motion. Her knees quivered as he guided her to the pool table.

"I think we're going to have to frisk her, boss," one guy said, meeting them at the table. "She could be carrying."

"My thoughts exactly," the leader agreed, giving her a little push until her breasts were flat out on the pool table.

Someone grabbed her hands and held them on the table above her head while a foot moved between her ankles to kick them open. Spread wide and completely at their mercy, she felt a big pair of hands on her legs. They slid all the way up one thigh, coming perilously close to her pussy before sliding down the other leg. Once complete, the guy ran his palms up her sides, stroking the edges of her breasts.

A small sound caught in her throat, and she tried again, "I'm looking for someone."

She was lifted from the table and spun to face the leader. "You're in luck. You've found someone." Two guys stepped up to her, caging her with their bodies. She caught a flash of silver, and her heart leapt as her Jackson look-alike pulled a knife from his pocket.

She opened her mouth to speak, but he shook his head to silence her. He ran the knife down the length of her dress, then began popping the buttons with the sharp tip. She compressed her lips as the buttons clattered to the floor and rolled away. Her dress began to spill open, exposing her nakedness beneath. Biker dude cut away her last button, and her safe word lingered on her tongue when he straightened to his full height, his eyes locking on hers.

"Tie her up," he ordered.

* * *

What the fuck was she doing here?

Jesse moved deeper into the shadows. He paced restlessly and mumbled a few curses as fellow biker, Keegan Gates, a guy he'd met when he first arrived, gave Alaska a pat down. Fisting his hands, he drove them into his pockets and fought for a measure of control. But how the fuck was he supposed to get his shit together, especially after watching her perform on the dock last evening? He might be the guy giving her the opportunity to live out her deepest, darkest desires, but watching her with those two jocks last night had damn near killed him. As they touched her, he couldn't help but imagine it was his tongue circling her pale nubs, coming closer and closer to her coveted peaks. Couldn't help but visualize it was his cock inside her, driving her higher and higher until her body exploded with pleasure. What he'd do to feel her come on *his* dick, to know that he was the guy giving her what she needed.

Last night it had taken every ounce of strength he had not to dive into the water, go to her, and claim her as his. At the last second, he'd somehow miraculously stopped himself from acting on his urges. As much as he wanted to climb onto that wharf and give her the fuck she always wanted from him—the fuck he always wanted to give her—he knew it was all kinds of wrong. Not because her father would kill him—hell, he was ready to stand up to her bastard father—but because, since the first time he met her, he knew that if he ever really touched her, ever drove his cock into her, he'd want more.

From the way she eyed his body, he knew Alaska wanted a piece of him, but he was a nobody, some punk-ass kid raised on the streets. A beautiful, intelligent girl like Alaska had a bright future ahead of her, providing she got out from under her father's hold, and deserved more than Jesse could ever give her.

He grabbed his beer, took a long pull, then slammed it on the oak bar top with much more force than necessary. The bartender gave him a questioning look, but he ignored it, all the while trying to fight down the lust rising in him. He'd come to this club tonight to cool his heels, to get his shit together. The last thing he ever expected was to find was Alaska walking through the front door of a gang's hangout. This was his sanctuary, goddammit, and she wasn't supposed to be here. As he chewed on that, another thought struck. Perhaps *this* was one of her fantasies. Or perhaps someone in charge was fucking with *him.*

Or maybe, just maybe, in some twisted, fucked up way, fantasy was tangling with reality.

One of Keegan's guys walked her to the middle of the room, where a rope hung from the rafters. He bound Alaska's hands, putting her naked body on view for every biker in the club to admire. Exhibitionist that she was, she nibbled her bottom lip as Keegan walked around her, lightly trailing his hands over her body. When he gave her ass a good hard smack, she made a whimpering sound that roused the hunger in him.

Feeling like he'd been sucker punched as another man stroked her and a handful more ogled her, a storm roiled inside Jesse. He fisted his hand, but the flash of possessiveness cutting though his gut like a sharp blade nearly brought him to his knees.

Fuck.

He finished off his beer and bit back another heated curse as he watched another man take what he wanted. His gaze shifted restlessly, moving over her beautiful, naked body. Jesus, she was so sexy, so sensual, so fucking impossible to resist.

Her glance moved over the room, searching the crowd. When she looked in his direction, he stiffened. Something in his gut warned that she knew he was here.

Keegan lowered his head, and when he took her nipple into his mouth, Jesse just about went out of his fucking mind. His body trembled, and he wasn't sure how much more he could take before he imploded. Keegan sucked her long and hard, and a look of desire moved over her face. She made a sexy noise, and Keegan inched back. He removed his belt, folded it, and stepped behind her. The snap of leather hitting her soft flesh cut through the room as he gave her a light whack on the ass.

Her mouth opened and closed, and when her nipples quivered, Jesse's mind practically shut down. Aware of the passion rising in him and completely ruled by lust, his mind abandoned any rational thought. As he watched Keegan touch her, every reason he had for staying away from her suddenly seemed insignificant.

Knowing he was fighting a losing battle, he adjusted his leather beanie cap over his forehead and tugged on the bandana around his neck, pulling it over his nose. Once his features were masked, he pushed off the counter, his vision a red hot blur of desire as he stalked toward her. His cock ached as he circled the room, quietly coming up behind Keegan. He tapped Keegan on the shoulder, and Keegan turned around to give Jesse a questioning look. With a flick of his head, Jesse gestured for him to back the fuck off. Keegan stepped away, leaving Jesse in charge of Alaska's pleasure and pain.

With his features hidden, he reached out and touched her back, lightly trailing his fingers down her spine. That first sweet touch of her nakedness had air rushing from his lungs. Her body quaked beneath his fingers, and he sucked in a fueling breath. Her skin was so damn soft, so warm it fired his blood from a slow simmer to a raging inferno.

He stepped closer, and she drew a small, shaky breath, her body visually quivering, and he realized that she might not be okay, that she might actually be afraid. Did she want out of this? He put his mouth close to her ear, the sweet scent of her hair twisting his insides.

"Are you afraid?" he asked, pitching his voice low.

Her body went suddenly stiff, like she knew the players had changed.

She breathed deep and exhaled slowly. "No," she answered in a soft whisper that made his blood rush. "I could never be afraid of you."

"You want this?"

"I want you," she said and moved her hips, relaxing under his touch, driving every sane thought from his brain. Her ass brushed up against his cock, feeding the intensity of his arousal as she urged him on.

As moisture collected on his brow, he clenched down on his jaw, working to keep it together when all he wanted to do was grab her by the hips and ram his cock into her. It frightened him how badly he wanted to fuck her, to bury his face in the heat between her legs. He closed his eyes against the flood of heat and worked to leash his control. Now that he had her where he'd always wanted her, he didn't want to rush anything.

Knowing just what sweet little Alaska needed, he slid his hands over her bare skin, his movements slow, deliberate, as he caressed the lush curves of her ass. She arched into him, and he pulled his hand back to give her a light whack.

With her body trembling, she let loose a little whimper, her head falling forward. He soothed her with his hands, then gave her another whack, a little harder this time, and she cried out. Jesus, he loved the way she reacted, how she let go of every inhibition and gave herself over to him.

He gripped her chin from behind and tilted her head back until it rested against his shoulder. He put lips to her ear. "You like that, do you?" he whispered.

Instead of answering, she squirmed, tucking her bottom up against him. He gripped her hips and held her still. If she kept that up, he was liable to shoot off in his pants before they even got started. "I wonder what other punishment you might like."

He grabbed a bandana from his back pocket and tied it around her head, taking care to cover her eyes. Once her vision was obscured, he pulled his own bandana from his face and walked around her, trailing his hands over her flesh. As his mind sifted through all the ways he wanted to pleasure her, to take her beyond her wildest fantasies, he walked to the bar, leaving her standing there in a quivering mess as he ordered a whiskey on the rocks.

With everyone in the room staring at Alaska and waiting to see what he had in store for her, he swallowed a mouthful of alcohol, then jangled the ice in the glass. The sound cut through the quiet. Alaska turned her head toward it, her mouth opening as she drew in a breath.

"What...what are you doing?" she whimpered. Jesse couldn't help but grin when he caught the anticipation in her voice.

"You don't get to ask the questions," he answered, taking charge.

As she made a mewling sound, he tossed an ice cube into his mouth and captured it in his front teeth. He moved into her space and dipped his head, running the ice down the long column of her neck until he reached her breasts. He circled one nipple, and she shivered almost violently in response.

"Oh, God," she cried out.

The ice melted fast on her hot skin, and he swallowed the liquid in his mouth. "You really are a bad girl, aren't you?" he murmured.

"Please…"

His dick throbbed, and tension rose in him as her pale nipples hardened, her body so needy for him. He fished another ice cube from his glass and swiped it over her other breasts. He greedily pulled her cold nipple into his mouth, blood pounding through his veins as he let the ice dissolve on her hard peak. Inching back, he tossed another cube into his mouth and brushed it over her stomach until it melted. He dipped lower, then went back on his heels to see her pretty pussy.

He widened her soft lips with his fingers, and as he took in her sweet pinkness, she squirmed. He held her still and nearly came unhinged as he breathed in the tang of her arousal. From the corner of his eyes, he spotted someone moving toward them to join in the fun, but seeing Alaska this excited, this needy for him, had his cock throbbing and possessiveness flashing through him. Like an animal marking its territory, he growled, and the guy backed off. What the fuck was she doing to him? Everything in the primal way he wanted her had him acting crazy, out of character. But he knew this was the only time he could ever have her, and he wasn't about to share.

He had no time to think about that right now, not when he was dying to taste her. Leaning in, he ran his ice cold tongue over her clit, and pleasure forked through him as she bucked against his mouth. Her scent curled around him, and the way her pussy glistened in the dim, overhead light was enough to shred his last ounce of control.

The lust that had been bottled up for months broke through the surface, and he suddenly found himself hungering for so much more. As her heat reached out to him and seeped under his skin, a fierce shudder overtook him.

With his body practically shaking and raw want ruling his actions, he pressed his mouth hungrily to her sex in an urgent exploration. He licked and sucked, yet still couldn't get enough of her. She squirmed beneath his mouth, and he damn near lost it when he slipped a finger inside to find her so tight…so fucking wet.

His cock strained against his zipper and a slow burn worked its way through his body to settle deep in his groin. He pressed another heated kiss over her pussy as his thumb circled her soaked clit. With his cock throbbing, he swirled a finger through her slick heat, and she thrust her pelvis harder against him.

"Easy, baby," he whispered with effort as the air around them grew heavy, saturated in lust as the others silently watched on. He lifted his head to see her, wishing he could look into her eyes when he made her come. Her mouth opened and closed as he dove back in to ravage her hot cunt, raw hunger consuming him. He licked her clit and slid another finger inside her. Her muscles bunched as she moved her hips, fucking him feverishly.

"That's it, baby," he murmured, and he brushed the tips of his fingers over her sensitive bundle of nerves. "Ride my fingers."

She gasped, and as he applied pressure to her clit, he could feel her legs buckle, tension building inside her. Knowing she was close, he finger fucked her a little faster, dying for her to come so he could taste her. She whimpered, her muscles contracting as she tumbled into orgasm, her liquid heat drenching his mouth. He kept his tongue on her cunt, drinking her in as she rode out the waves. Jesus Christ, he'd never tasted anything sweeter.

He lapped up every last drop, then, desperate to be inside her, he eased away and drew a ragged breath. With his heart hammering, he climbed to his feet and worked to keep his hands from trembling when he looked at Keegan.

His nostrils flared, and it took effort to disguise his voice when he commanded, "Untie her hands and bend her over the pool table."

Alaska squirmed as Keegan unhooked her hands. Keegan caught her trembling body and carried her to the table. Pressure brewed deep in Jesse's groin as his body registered every delicious detail of the girl he was about to fuck senseless: her hair tumbling in waves over the felt table top, her sweet ass up in the air, her body so open, so ready for him.

As he stalked across the room, he couldn't think about the line he was crossing or that they had no future together when they left this island. No, as he stepped up to her, running his hands over her ass, all he could think about was getting his cock inside her and fucking long into the night. Every night.

Bombarded with hunger, he ripped open his pants and shoved them down his thighs. After quickly rolling on a condom, he gripped her hips, slipped his legs between hers, and urged her thighs apart. With her ass tipped up so nicely and her damp pussy glistening in the overhead light, he positioned his cock at her hot entrance, ready to ram it home. Lacking any sort of finesse and concerned only about getting inside her, he powered his hips forward, and with one fierce thrust, sank into her warm, wet heat.

"Holy fuck," he moaned as her muscles closed around him, her pussy hugging his cock so tight, he almost fucking lost it. Fire pitched through him as he pulled back and rammed again, wanting…needing…more. Breath rushed from his lungs as he speared her, and she rocked with him, establishing a rhythm as he angled his body for deeper, harder thrusts.

Panting like a damn animal, he fucked her, using long, hard strokes to go balls deep, yet still unable to get enough of him inside her.

"So good," she cried out, opening herself to him.

He loved how she responded to him, the satisfaction in her voice, and was thrilled to know that he could do this to her, even though she had no idea it was him. The more he thought about it, the more he realized that he couldn't recall her responding so wildly, so open, to any of the guys she'd been paired with so far. Her fingers clawed at the table, and even though some small coherent part of his brain told him he shouldn't be doing this, it felt so fucking good, so right to be inside her.

Restraint a thing of the past, he rode her furiously, his cock moving urgently inside her. He bucked forward, slipped a hand between her legs, and applied gentle pressure to the spot that made her moan the loudest.

He clenched down on his jaw, struggling to hang on, but the second she came again, her cream searing his cock, he lost it. Leaning over her, he gripped her shoulders, and with one final thrust, he gave himself over to his own orgasm. He shot off inside her, his body trembling from head to toe as his cock pulsed and spasmed, depleting every ounce of cum inside her hot cunt.

As her throaty purr resonated through his body, he knew he needed one kiss. Just one tiny, little kiss. With everything in him aching to taste the sweetness of her mouth, he pulled out of her, picked her up off the table, and spun her around, desperate to taste her mouth. Her hair flared as she turned to face him. With the bandana still around her eyes, he pressed her ass against the pool table, his hands holding hers against her hips as his mouth crashed down on hers. He pushed his tongue inside, slashing it against the inside of her cheeks as he devoured her like a man starved for more than just sex. She pulled her hands from his and slid them around his body, touching him like she couldn't get enough as she kissed him back. The intensity in what he felt for her scared the shit out of him. Electricity arched between them, and after a thorough taste of her mouth, he broke the kiss, leaving her lips bruised as she gasped for breath.

Panting heavily, he pulled his bandana back up and managed to mask his identity seconds before she tugged hers down. Their glances clashed and the dark desire he met in her gaze nearly unglued him.

His heart raced, pounding, apprehension building inside him. Everything in the way she looked at him, recognition dancing in her eyes, told him she knew. She knew all along it was him.

"Jesse," she murmured.

As the lust cleared and reality came rushing back in a *whoosh*, he took a distancing step back. Shit, he knew he never should have fucked her, gone at her like a goddamn rutting animal. Hadn't he warned himself that if he ever touched her, kissed her, put his cock inside her, that he'd want more? This was a dangerous game he was playing, and if he knew what was good for him, he'd end this shit right now.

CHAPTER SEVEN

Alaska tossed restlessly in her bed, trying to come to some explanation as to why Jesse had taken off after giving her the best sex of her life, distancing himself both physically and emotionally before she could talk to him. But she needed answers…needed to know if he was the guy responsible for this vacation. And if so, why? She thought back to the contest question and how easy it was for her to answer. Jesse was one of the few people who knew how much she loved to dance. Even though all clues pointed to him, the price tag associated with a fantasy vacation like this gave her a measure of doubt. She was sure a week on Eden would cost way more than he made in an entire year.

She looked outside her window to see a multi-colored bird perched on her sill. As it sang to her, she thought back to the way Jesse had touched her, and her body tightened with the memories. She felt his presence in the bar long before he came to her. When the players had changed and she caught the distinctive smell of his skin, felt the intensity in his touch, she knew it was Jesse touching her body.

Her body throbbed as she recalled the way his fingers stroked her with hunger, the way he kissed her with need, and even though he'd been disguising his voice, it still did mysterious things to her nerves.

Alaska threw off her blankets and climbed to her feet, determined to find him before the day was over. If he continued to avoid her, then she'd have no choice but to figure out a way to draw him out. Because she wanted answers, and she wanted them now.

A quick shower later, she pulled on another one of her sundresses then stepped out into the warm sunshine. She walked the beach and passed the Tiki bar and the washroom/changing area, noticing that someone had left the outdoor rain shower on. After turning it off, she made her way to one of the many paths and flagged down a driver.

He dropped her off at the pavilion, and as she explored, walking around the people checking emails on the lounge sofas, she once again found herself near the stage, watching the dancers practicing for their nightly show. She studied them for a second longer and was about to leave before the director kicked her out again, when one of the girl's sank to the floor, gripping her ankle.

Caleb dropped down next to her, and after a quick examination, he carried her off the stage. He set her in a chair in the front row, motioned for the director, then glanced up to see Alaska.

"Janey," he called out, a big smile on his face as he waved her over.

Alaska walked down the aisle toward the stage and looked at the girl soothing her foot. "Are you okay?" she asked, knowing how bad an ankle injury could be for a dancer.

"I think it's sprained," she said.

The director jumped off the stage, and a medic came

with his bag. The two attended to the girl as Caleb pulled Alaska away.

"I've been looking for you," he said, his dark eyes glistening.

She gave a small smile and said, "I've been a bit busy."

"Well, I'm glad you finally came to talk." He cocked his head, his eyes hopeful. "Does this mean you're going to dance for us?"

She shook her head. "I'm only here for a few more days."

He shot the injured dancer a glance, and Alaska cringed as the medic wrapped a bandage around her ankle. "Now that Emma's laid up, we'll need a replacement."

"I—"

Before he could give her a chance to say no, he gripped her hips, lifted her clear off her feet, and sat her on the stage. He jumped up beside her and pulled her to her feet as the music started up.

She stood there staring at the dancers, at Caleb, hardly able to believe what was going on.

"Dance with me, Janey," he said, pressing his body to hers.

"I'm not sure—"

"I am."

As everyone looked at her with hopeful eyes, her resolve melted. They all seemed to be counting on her to fill the vacant position so they could continue to practice, and since she didn't want to let them down, she whispered, "Just this once."

Caleb shrugged. "If you say so."

He grabbed her hand to set her into motion. Thankful that she'd seen enough of the routine to follow along for the most part, she took her place in line. As she kicked up her legs, she knew she could perfect the moves with a little more practice.

Deciding to go for it, to just let go and enjoy this for what it was, she let Caleb take the lead and danced with him. Feeling alive and free as he spun her around, she soon found herself laughing and enjoying every minute of the performance. As Caleb pulled her close, she looked at all the empty seats facing the stage and imagined what it would be like to dance for a captive audience. What it would be like to live here on the island and be a part of this dance troupe?

When the song ended, Caleb pressed his lips to her cheek. "The job's yours," he said, like he knew what she was thinking. Then again, it was like everyone here knew what she wanted, needed, including Jack and Blair. It made her wonder if they were staff, too.

Breathing hard she said, "Caleb, I can't."

He smiled. "You're on Eden, Janey. The word *can't* doesn't exist." She looked at the dancers, then glanced around. "Staff are treated exceptionally well," he continued and opened his arms wide. "Everything you could ever want, you'll find on Eden."

Truthfully, right now what she wanted was to find Jesse. She just needed to figure out a way how.

"So what do you say?" he asked as he tossed her a towel.

She blotted her cheeks, and in an effort to appease him, she said, "I'll think about it." After handing him back the towel, she jumped down from the stage and continued her search. As she walked through the breakfast area, Caleb's words continued to ring in her mind.

As wonderful as joining the troupe would be, she couldn't just disappear and lose herself in Eden, could she? Then again, what kind of life was she going back to? One on lockdown with a father who cared nothing about her—had so much as abandoned her—and a mother who left her to fend for herself when she was just a child.

Before she could give it any more thought, the hairs on her nape began to tingle, and she knew Jesse was here, watching her. Had he been watching her perform, too?

Her glance surfed through the crowd, and her mind raced, taking her back to her dorm and the night he walked in on her when she was masturbating. She'd seen his reactions, the need in his body. A small grin tugged at her mouth, because she suddenly knew just what she had to do to get him to come to her. Oh yeah, she wasn't the only one with fantasies.

* * *

Jesse raked his hair off his face as he walked the beach, wondering what Alaska's fantasy might be tonight and how he was going to make it through it without losing his mind. He'd avoided her today, but he didn't miss seeing her dance or the joy on her face as she performed with the troupe. Dancing was her life, what she was meant to do. If she followed that dream, she was definitely going to go places and find happiness.

He, on the other hand, was just a punk-ass kid with skills for fighting. The streets were his home, and he had no way off them, no way to get out from under Franco's hold. He'd never really given his future much thought. When a guy went day-to-day, he never knew if he'd have another one. But now, after watching Alaska for so long, after she gave herself to him last night, he couldn't help but imagine what it would be like to make things between them more permanent. Except he couldn't allow himself the luxury of thinking about that. They'd be back at the dorm in a few short days, and he wasn't going to drag her to the gutters with him. No, she was going places, and he wasn't going to stand in her way.

As night fell over Eden, he searched the island for her. There were no nightclubs in the sky, no carousels, no couples in the middle of a scene. He checked the dock, the motorcycle club, and even the dance stage, but she was nowhere to be found, none of her fantasies taking place. Unease moved into his stomach. Where the hell was she?

Fighting down the panic churning in his gut, he hurried to her cabana. He knocked, but when no answer came, he kicked open the door. He did a thorough search of her room, even checking the bathroom. He hurried back outside and scanned the shoreline, the last place he'd seen her. She was his responsibility, and if anything ever happened to her… Jesus, he couldn't finish that thought. The truth was his fear for her safety had nothing to do with his role as her protector and everything to do with the way he felt about her.

With his pulse racing and knowing security patrolled the beaches to prevent uninvited visitors from sneaking onto Eden, he ran along beach, his steps slowing as he passed the now empty Tiki bar. Where was everyone? The sound of water drew his attention, and he cautiously moved toward the changing areas.

When he spotted Alaska standing beneath the outdoor rain shower, warm water rushing down her beautiful, naked body, his heart nearly stopped. She ran her hands through her hair, the sweet floral scent of her shampoo calling out to him in mind-fucking ways. Unable to help himself, he stood in the shadows and watched her. His stomach tensed. It suddenly occurred to him that she knew more about him than he ever realized, which begged the question, did she know who he really was?

He took in the look on her face, the honesty and openness she displayed as she finished washing her hair and aimed the spray between her legs. She touched herself, her fingers sliding over her clit, and his mouth watering for another taste.

Her full lips parted, and she made a sexy bedroom noise. His cock instantly hardened.

Walk away, Jesse.

She ran her fingers over her hard nipples, and heat flashed through him, making it impossible to move.

Her lashes blinked open, and when she aimed a small, inviting smile his way, like she knew he was there, he stepped from the shadows. They exchanged a long, heated look, one that had him hungering for so much from her. As she baited him, knowing just what he liked and how he liked it, he took another step toward her.

What the fuck are you doing, dude?

She crooked her finger, and as she urged him closer, he groaned low in his throat.

"What are you doing?" he asked.

"What we should have done that first night. We've wasted so much time," she whispered, her voice so soft and low he had to strain to hear it.

Her glance left his face and, with excruciating slowness, moved over his body. As he watched her eyes dim with desire, a slow burn worked its way through his blood. He so was fucked. Totally and utterly fucked.

As they came full circle, and she offered her body up to him so nicely, giving him complete control, he could no longer think with clarity. He stepped under the shower fully clothed and packaged her body against his. His nostrils flared, and he dipped his head, his lips so close to hers. He exhaled a shallow breath, picked her up off the floor, and backed her up until she was caged between his chest and the shower wall.

He pushed his cock against her pussy and said, "Is this what you want?"

CHAPTER EIGHT

"You're what I want," she whispered as his lips crashed down on hers.

"Then I should give you what you want," he growled into her mouth, his deep, tortured tone sending a barrage of erotic sensations through her.

Alaska tore at his shirt, desperate to get her hands on him, to feel his bare skin against hers. "I need you naked," she said, her fingers moving urgently, like her world would end if she couldn't get his clothes off fast enough.

He dropped his head against hers, took a breath, and let it out slowly. His words were soft when he whispered, "Not here."

Her heart lurched. Was he having second thoughts?

He have a hard shake and turned the water off. "Not like this."

Without speaking, he picked up her naked body and carried her across the beach to her cabana. He pushed through her door and flicked on the light with his elbow. Carrying her to her bed, he gently tossed her down and stood there for a moment, looking at her.

As she lay there, completely exposed, he tore off his shirt and shorts, and when he looked back at her, she could see the tender side of her biker boy. Her heart swelled, needing him more now than she ever did.

"Like this," he said as he climbed on the bed and, with finesse, gently opened her thighs. "Because I need to see you when you come."

She let loose a strangled cry. "Oh, God," she whispered, hardly able to believe the guy she'd wanted for so long was here with her, was interested in giving her more than a hard, quick fuck in the shower.

He slipped between her legs and licked her. He tasted slowly, like he was savoring her flavor, enjoying feeling her heat, her wetness on his tongue. He licked and nibbled, slowly building her orgasm, slowly making her crazed. She arched into him, her hands raking through his hair as she ground herself against his mouth.

His thumb probed her opening, and every nerve ending in her body came alive. She moved under him, writhing on the sheets as he pillaged her with his mouth.

"So good," she cried out.

Her clit quivered under his artful manipulation, and he deepened the kiss as he pushed one thick finger all the way inside her.

He growled and looked up at her. She went up on her elbows, knowing he wanted to see her face when she came for him. The way he looked at her with pure desire made her insides quiver.

"Jesse..." she croaked out when their eyes met and locked. They exchanged a long, heated look, and the raw need in his eyes squeezed the air from her lungs. Oh, God, she was so crazy about the tough boy who was as lonely and lost as her. Her body tightened, everything inside her fluttering as she gave herself over to him.

He pressed another finger inside her, slowly building her orgasm. Even though she could sense his urgency, he took his time with her. He knew just how to touch her, just how to take her higher and higher.

Her entire body moistened, her nipples aching for his attention. As if sensitive to her needs, he moved a thumb to her clit and climbed up her body, his mouth closing around one hard bud. She sucked in a tight breath as he bit down on her, then used his tongue to soothe the sting left behind.

A whimper bubbled in her throat as he touched her with such tender care. In no time at all, a surge of warmth flooded her veins, and her pussy clenched around his fingers. She pinched her eyes shut. "Jesse," she cried out, her voice trembling with the same intensity as her body.

"Look at me," he said.

Her lids fluttered open, and her heart turned over in her chest when she caught the possessive way he stared back.

He applied more pressure to her clit, and her skin grew tight. He found the sensitive bundle of nerves inside her and circled them, urging her on. He slowly built her orgasm, taking her places only he had ever taken her before. As tension grew in her core, she gripped his shoulders, connecting more than just their bodies.

"Jesse," she whimpered, her throat closing over as everything she felt for him rushed to her heart.

"I know, baby. I know."

With a new intimacy between them, she wrapped her arms around him and gave herself over to the pleasure. Her mouth opened, but no words came as her pussy spasmed, her hot release more powerful than anything she'd ever felt.

"Jesus," he growled, his nostrils flaring as he held her tight, his muscles absorbing her tremors.

When her body settled, he put his mouth close to hers

and said, "I need to be inside you."

"First, I need to do something," she said, her mouth watering for him.

A look of confusion moved over his face as she shoved him, pushing him until he was flat on his back. Once she had him where she wanted him, she positioned herself between his legs.

"Oh, fuck," he cried out as she bent forward to run her tongue over his crown, sampling the precum dripping from his slit. She pulled him into her mouth, relaxing her throat, but could barely take even half of him in. He fisted her hair, and his hands followed the motion as she slid him in and out of her mouth, loving the taste and texture of his skin.

The veins in his shaft filled with heated blood, and she cupped his balls to give them a gentle massage.

"Baby," he said, a desperate edge to his voice as he pulled back. "You're going to make me come, and I'm not ready for that."

He grabbed his shorts from the floor, pulled out a condom, and quickly sheathed himself. Climbing back on top of her, his weight pressing her into the mattress in the most erotic ways as his cock found her opening. He pushed into her, burrowing deep and filling her in a way no man ever had before.

They rocked together, both giving and taking as they shut out the world, concerned only about each other. His mouth took possession of hers, and in no time at all, she became lost in the moment, the sensations…Jesse. Everything in the way he touched her, kissed her, took their relationship to a whole new level.

Their first time together, the scene in the motorcycle club, had been pure lust. This was different. Last night, Jesse's hands had been rough on her, bringing pleasure from pain. Now they smoothed over her skin with a gentleness that stole her breath. Where the night before his voice had been raw and commanding, tonight he whispered dark words of encouragement as his mouth moved over her flesh. He pumped harder, the depth of penetration stealing her breath and building the tension inside her. His muscles bunched as he slipped a hand between their bodies and stroked her with expertise. Alaska's body responded with a violent shudder, followed by another mind-blowing orgasm. As her liquid heat coated his cock, he groaned, pulled all the way out, and with one hard thrust, drove back into her. She held him tight, raking her nails over his back as he pulsed inside her, his cock spasming and throbbing as he succumbed to the pressure.

"Fuck," he murmured and collapsed on top of her, their collective orgasms leaving them both shaken, gasping for breath.

Moisture sealed them as one as they held one another. The thought that she'd like to stay like this forever slipped into her head, but he rolled off and pulled her to him. His warm familiarity curled around her, and she exhaled a contented breath, never wanting to leave the circle of his arms.

She looked up at him, everything in her heart telling her this was more than a purely physical relationship. His touch was different from the other guys she was with. It was less physical, more emotional. Whether Jesse wanted to admit to it or not, they'd made love...made a connection. His interest in her went deeper than a wild night of sex. The way he put her needs first proved that.

When he caught the way she was looking at him, his mouth found hers again, and the remainder of the night was lost in a haze of sleep and lovemaking. Soon the sun crested the horizon, and with exhaustion pulling at them both, she cuddled into him. She touched his face, wanting to talk, but a loud noise outside the cabana had him jumping to his feet. Eyes hard, he tugged on his clothes and gave her a warning glance.

"Stay here."

Seeing that he was in protective mode, ready for a fight, she nodded and drew her blankets up. Jesse eased open the door, shot her one last glace, and then disappeared.

With the sun rising, she wrapped her blanket around her and climbed from the bed. Heart racing, she peeked through her curtains in time to see Jesse take a man down in the sand. His movements were swift and sure as he pressed his knee into the small of the man's back and rendered him immobile while the intruder's friends in a nearby speedboat took off and left him to fend for himself. She looked down the beach and spotted security running toward Jesse.

Jesse took his knee off the guy's back and handed him off to security. They spoke for a few minutes, then the Master of the island showed up. The two walked the length of the beach as they talked. Alaska watched them until they walked into the tree line and disappeared from sight. She sat on the edge of her bed, waiting for him to return. After an hour had passed, and Jesse still hadn't returned, she got up, got dressed, and went to find him. She found him at the far end of the beach, sitting alone on the sand, his knees to his chest, his arms wrapped around them, as he stared out at the sun rising over the ocean.

His body tensed as she approached, and the wind blew his hair from his face. She stood for a moment, and when he failed to acknowledge her presence, she carefully lowered herself beside him, mimicking his position. Half expecting him to tell her to go, Alaska sat quietly and gave him some time. After a while, when he still didn't speak, she turned to him, resting her cheek on her knees.

"Why did you do this, Jesse?" The only sign that he'd heard her was a slight tightening of his shoulders. So stubborn. She leaned over, nudging him with her elbow. Finally, he tipped his head and looked at her. "Why did you bring me here?"

"Janey—" he began, then stopped when she arched a brow. He huffed out a half-laugh and shook his head. "You think you know everything, don't you?"

"Not everything, but I do know that you arranged all of this." She shifted, lifted her head, and propped her chin on her knees. "And I know who you are."

His gaze returned to the horizon. "How long have you known?"

"I've always known." Unable to help herself, she reached out, running her fingers along his tattoos. He flinched at first but then relaxed into her touch. "But what I want to know is why. Why did you do this?"

He shrugged and shot her a quick look when he said, "Because you were sad, so lonely. I wanted to do this for you."

Her heart went into her throat. Even though she didn't want to pry, she couldn't help but ask, "How did you afford all this?"

"I sold my bike."

She sucked in air. "Jesse…"

"It's no big deal."

Her fingers shook as she linked them together. "I can't believe you did that for me."

"Look, I brought you here for you." The muscle in his jaw ticked. "I wasn't supposed to get personally involved in your fantasies."

"Then why did you?"

"Because…"

"Because why?"

"I care about you, Alaska," he said quietly. "That's why I volunteered for the job of watching over you." He frowned and his mouth clamped shut like he wanted to take his words back, like he'd said too much.

"You…you volunteered?"

He glanced away. "Yeah."

"I had no idea. I thought you were picked because you were young and could fit in at the dorm."

"It's no big deal."

"It is to me."

"I just hated the way your father treated you." His hand went to the scrolls on his arms. "And I swore…" He stopped, letting his words fall off.

"Tell me," she urged.

"I wanted to protect you from your father. No girl should ever suffer abuse from their father," he said and she sensed he was talking from personal experience.

She put her hand over his, her eyes going to the tattoo scrolls. She looked closer, and her stomach tightened when she saw all the scars camouflaged beneath the black ink. "Did your father do this?"

When his glance lifted from his tattoos to her, the vulnerability Alaska saw there caught her heart in a vice. His mouth worked, as if he wanted to say something but was holding back. He looked away again and pressed his lips together. After a moment, in a voice so soft the ocean breeze almost took it, he said, "Yeah."

Tears burned the backs of Alaska's lids. She blinked them away. "And you have a sister?"

Jesse nodded, his eyes moving over the horizon as if seeing the past. "She was older, and I was too little. I…couldn't protect her."

Alaska swallowed the lump forming in her throat. "Where is she now?"

His chest rose on an intake of breath. "Drug overdose." Expression pained, he stretched his legs out before him. Alaska looked into his eyes and glimpsed the inner man, so well hidden behind a tough exterior.

"The streets were hard on her," he said quietly.

Alaska climbed to her feet. As he looked up at her, she lowered herself onto his lap, straddling his hips, needing to connect with him more than ever. Her lips came down on his, and her hands cupped his face when she whispered into his mouth, "They were hard on you, too."

* * *

His heart pounded as Alaska kissed him, her mouth so warm, her body so welcoming. She broke the kiss and inched back, her eyes moving over his face, her fingers touching his scars. Jesse's throat constricted. He could hardly believe that he'd open up to her so easily, sharing his painful past. He'd never talked to anyone else about it. As he looked up at her now, the walls he'd built to protect himself came crashing down. Everything in the way she looked back at him, with desire, trust, and respect, sent new life surging through his veins. He felt…comforted. He'd never had that before. There had never been anyone who had cared enough to give it. Was it possible…?

"I want you inside me," she whispered, "But first, this."

She slid down his legs and pulled his cock from his shorts. He kept his eyes on hers as she stroked him, running her hands up and down the length of him until he was rock solid. Once she had him where she wanted him, she leaned in and took him in her mouth.

Jesse threw his head back, enjoying the feel of her wet tongue on him, the softness in her touch, the closeness he felt with her.

She licked him and his body convulsed, needing to bury himself inside her as she drew him in to a place where emotions ruled.

Perspiration beaded his forehead, and he swiped it. "Alaska, baby, you don't have to…" he murmured.

She lifted her head and gave him a warm smile. "I like the way you say my name."

His heart squeezed as her words triggered a craving he'd never before experienced. "Come here." He put one hand around her neck, and his pulse pounded in his throat as he pulled her to his mouth. He kissed her long and deep, savoring the taste of her. He brushed her hair from her face and worked to find his voice. "I need to be inside you now."

She nodded, desire reflecting in her eyes as she peeled off her dress. Her eyes locked on his as she bared herself to him. It was as though she was offering more than just her body. He reached into his pocket and pulled out a condom. She took it from him, and he groaned as she tore it open and rolled it on. He gripped her hips and positioned her on top of him. She wiggled, but he held her tight, controlling the pace. He offered her an inch, and she moaned, trying to break free of his hold so she could impale herself.

Inch-by-inch he slid into her, until he was buried in her balls deep. Good God, she felt so good…so right. He cupped her breasts and gently stroked her nipples as she moved her hips, rocking into him.

Her hands went to his chest, and she lifted herself slightly, driving his cock in and out of her. Fuck, if she kept that up, he'd lose it in record time.

His mind shut down as they established a rhythm, and his fingers bit into her hips harder. Overcome with need, the things this girl made him feel, he powered his hips upward. As he stretched her, her fingers curled into his chest, and she made a soft, mewling sound. Her eyes clouded with desire, and tenderness stole over him, the need to take her higher and higher urging him on.

"You are so beautiful, Alaska," he murmured, his

cock throbbing inside her as she opened herself to him.

She gave him a genuine smile, and his heart twisted with the things she stirred inside him. He pushed impossibly deeper and reached between them to press his thumb to her clit. Her eyes flared hot, and he knew she was close…so close.

His throat dried. "I love when you come for me," he managed to say as everything inside him screamed possession. Love.

"Oh God, Jesse," she cried out as she arched her back, releasing all over his cock.

Her juice dripped to his balls, and they contracted against his body. "Fuck," he murmured, struggling to hang on as she rode out the waves.

She rocked her hips, and he closed his eyes against the flood of heat, his body screaming for release. "Please, Jesse," she cried out as if she could feel the tension rising in him. "Come with me."

Her muscles clenched around him and every working brain cell shut down, the only thing he could think about was this girl and how good it felt to be inside her, how he never wanted to be anywhere else. He gripped her hips, and his body trembled almost uncontrollably as he held her still and shot off inside her.

"Oh, fuck," he yelled, as he throbbed and stayed buried deep until he completely depleted himself in her. Her hands found his, and they threaded their fingers together. "Oh my God, Alaska." He pulled her hand to his mouth and gave it a kiss.

Her soft chuckle seeped under his skin. "Yeah, I know," she said, her eyes raking over him.

He inched out of her, discarded the condom, and pulled her down on top of him. Her body melted against his as she rested her head against his chest. Her lashes fluttered against his skin as her finger circled his nipple.

He exhaled slowly, feeling relaxed for the first time

in…hell, he'd never been this loose. God, if only they could stay like this forever. Everything in this situation felt natural, right.

There was no denying that he'd grown to care about Alaska. Had always cared about her, in fact, enough so that he was willing to take his chances with her father in order to bring her here.

But where did they go from here? In a few short days, they'd be going home, and he'd be stepping back into the role of bodyguard like nothing had changed.

Only problem was, now that he'd been with Alaska—been inside her—everything had changed.

CHAPTER NINE

Alaska stretched out on the sand beside Jesse. "It is so beautiful here."

"Yeah, it is."

"I still can't believe you did this for me." He felt her studying his profile as she breathed in the warm air and let it out slowly. "I knew there was a reason I always liked you."

He angled his head to see her. "You always liked me?"

She rolled her eyes at him. "Of course I did. Don't pretend you didn't know it, either."

"I guess I shouldn't be surprised," he teased as he flexed his muscles. "What's not to like?"

She went up on one elbow and turned toward him. "How come you never acted on what was between us?" She winked. "God knows I tried to get you to."

All humor fell from his eyes. "I'm not the guy for you," he said soberly.

Her head jerked back. "How can you say that?"

"You don't know me, Alaska."

"Then let me get to know you." When he went quiet,

she asked, "Are you afraid I won't like what I see?"

"I have nothing to offer you."

Her glance moved over his face, taking in the scars he couldn't hide with tattoos. "You're right," she said. "You were brought up in a horrible family, dragged up on the streets, and did what you had to do to survive. Really, you're nothing but a bike-riding street thug."

He flinched, and even though it was true, her words still stung. "Shit, why don't you tell me what you really think?"

"I'd rather tell you what I know."

"Go ahead, then. You know, since you seem to be on a roll and all."

"Well, what I know is that for a guy who had to face what you did, you turned out to be pretty damn amazing." He opened his mouth to cut her off, but she pressed her fingers to his lip and continued. "You're the first guy, the first person in my entire life, who ever cared about me. You actually risked your life to give me a bit of excitement. Honestly, no one has ever put my needs first, especially at the risk of losing their life." She shook her head. "Do you have any idea how much that means to me?" She trailed her fingers over his face, surfing the outline of his jaw. "But you're right, any guy who would do what you did for me certainly isn't the guy for me."

"Listen, Alaska. You have a bright future ahead of you, and you don't need a nobody like me dragging you down. In fact, when we go back home, I'm going to talk to your father. I'm going to tell him to let you live your own life."

She smiled and settled her palm on his cheek. "You'd do that for me?"

"I would," he said without hesitation. "And I will."

"You know what he'll do to you, right?"

"I don't care what he does to me, because I'm not

going to let him hold you back anymore."

She traced her hands over his tattoo. "Just for the record, Jesse, you're hardly a nobody. In fact, you're my hero. You set all of this up, arranged a week at this amazing place, just for me. You gave me the opportunity to free myself in so many ways, and you showed me what real intimacy is." She exhaled slowly and went back on her elbows. "And you should know, I'm not going back. I was offered a job dancing."

Shocked, he stiffened, but then he smiled, because the more he thought about it, the more he knew this was perfect. Here, she'd get out from under her father's control and live the life she wanted. "You're so happy when you're dancing."

"I would ask you to stay with me, but I know you'd eventually get bored and abandon me just like everyone else I've ever cared about."

Anger churned in his gut, and suddenly feeling very defensive, he shot back, "I took the job because I cared about your wellbeing. But the second I set eyes on you, I felt this jolt inside of me." He shook his head. "I never felt anything like that before. It was like…like…"

"Destiny?" she asked.

"I don't know, Alaska. All I know is that being so close to you, watching you every day, and not being able to touch you, kiss you, make you mine, damn near drove me out of my mind." He cupped her face. "I'm not like your parents and would never tire of you, never in a million years. Believe me, I want to stay. If you're not in Chicago, then there's no reason for me to go back."

"I guess that settles it then." She gave him a triumphant grin.

His head came back with a start, realizing she'd turned everything back around on him. "Wait, did you just…"

She grinned. "Yeah. I've been taking psychology as

my electives."

"Alaska, I have nothing…"

"You have me. Do you need anything more?"

They stared at each other for a long time, and as he thought about her fantasies, he suddenly couldn't stand the thoughts of another man's hands on her body. *He* wanted to be the last guy to touch her, care for her, give her everything she wanted.

His fingers found hers as something in him gave. "Why do you want me, Alaska?"

"When I first stepped foot on this island, I felt like Cinderella. But then I realized Prince Charming didn't exist because the men in my life were greedy and corrupt and cared only about themselves. You proved me wrong." She squeezed his fingers. *"You're* my Prince Charming."

"I'm no…"

"Yes, you are. Believe me. I know what I'm talking about."

There was a fire in her eyes that told him not to mess with her. "How?

"Because I believe in you."

He swallowed and thought back to his fucked up childhood, his days street fighting. "No one has ever believed in me before."

She nudged him playfully. "That's because you've been hanging out with the wrong people."

He grinned. "I should probably tell you that I was also offered a job here, as security."

The excited smile that she aimed his way nearly stopped his heart. "It's like this island knew what we needed long before we did."

"Yeah, you might be right about that," he said, thinking about how she crossed over into his reality at the motorcycle club.

Her eyes lit up with hope and joy. "So you'll stay

here." She waved her hand toward the beach. "We can disappear here together on Eden."

He pushed her hair from her face, his heart aching with all the things he felt for her. "Alaska, things won't be like they were. Your fantasy ends on the weekend. You know that right?"

She smiled at him, a smile so full of love and warmth his chest swelled until he could barely catch his breath. She leaned into him, her sweet scent overwhelming him as she pressed her lips to his, a soft kiss, a kiss full of love and promise.

"You're wrong, Jesse. My fantasy is just beginning."

"Yeah?" he murmured into her mouth, knowing everything he ever wanted was right in front of him.

"Yeah," she responded as she kissed him back.

Jesse pulled her in tighter. He might be a street thug, and she might be a mob boss's daughter, but together, they were both half of something pretty cool, something he'd be a damn fool to walk away from. "I believe mine is, too, Alaska," he murmured, deepening the kiss. "I believe mine is, too…"

OTHER INVITATION TO EDEN TITLES

Join my New Release Newsletter to be the first to hear about new releases and contests.
http://bit.ly/1kpQOzf

Like what you just read?
Make sure to check out the rest of
Invitation to Eden series.
Sign up for our mailing list http://eepurl.com/QvEdn
to receive new release alerts!
For more information about the island of Eden, check out our website http://www.invitationtoeden.com/

March
Master of the Island by Lauren Hawkeye

April
Random Acts of Fantasy by Julia Kent
Yours Truly, Taddy by Avery Aster
Escape From Reality by Adriana Hunter

May
Hydrotherapy by Suzanne Rock
Fight For Me by Sharon Page
His Fair Lady by Marian Tee

June
Breaking Free by Cathryn Fox
Hold Me Close by Eliza Gayle
Queen's Knight by Sara Fawkes

July
How To Tempt A Tycoon by Daire St. Denis

Dare to Surrender by Carly Phillips
The Capture by Erika Wilde

August
Rough Draft by Mari Carr
Blurring The Lines by Roni Loren
Return to Sender by Steena Holmes

September
Pleasure Point by Eden Bradley
Wild Ride by Opal Carew
Master of Pleasure by Lauren Hawkeye

October
Her Desert Heart by Delilah Devlin
Ivy in Bloom by Vivi Anna writing as Tawny Stokes
Thorne of a Rose by Kimberly Kaye Terry

November
Falling or Flying by R.G. Alexander
Elusive Hero by Joey W. Hill
Captive of Desire by Sarah Castille

December
Delicious and Deadly by C.C. MacKenzie
Pleasure Games by Jessica Clare
The Last Seduction by Jennifer Probst

INVITATION TO EDEN SNEAK PEEKS

Have you read Invitations to Eden's other June releases?

Hold Me Close by Eliza Gayle
(Purgatory Club, Book 6)

Sometimes you need to cut and run and sometimes the ties run too deep to abandon. Bonnie's job at Purgatory keeps her on edge in more ways than one. Every day the pain of her grief over losing her Dom threatens to consume her. Her only escape comes at the hands of the resident tattooed bad boy who likes to keep things light and loose with a variety of women. He may not be the Dom of her dreams, but he chases away the darkness if only for one night... Dex is used to unattached submissives coming to him for a chance to feel the kiss of his flogger or the sting of his whip until they find their own Doms. With his busy life of ink and kink he likes keeping his women at arm's length. Except one night a month when Bonnie shreds him every time she asks him to hold her close. When a secret invitation to an island resort arrives, is it the answer to their problems? Or their worst nightmare?

Queen's Knight by Sara Fawkes
(a story set in the Anything He Wants world)

A man for whom Dominance is a way of life. A woman who refuses to yield control. Dany McQueen was good at her job, and she knew it. Being the PA to one of New York's most respected professional Doms had it's unique challenges, but she could handle anything thrown her way...except the invitation to participate. Giving up control scared her, even when the offer was tempting beyond belief. When an invitation turns up at her door, however, that may give her a chance to live out her deepest fantasy, she's ready to give it a shot. Gabriel Knight was getting old, and he felt every year. With his latest sub ending their partnership to pursue a vanilla relationship and family, he's suddenly loathe to take on any more trainees. When his long-time personal assistant requests a vacation, he's more than willing to grant it…until he realized exactly where she is going. Dany thought Eden would be somewhere she could enjoy her fantasies, safe from the pressure of her real life. She never expected for her boss to follow her, nor that his relentless pursuit would awaken a desire inside her she'd refused to allow herself before. Now that she's had a taste of her Knight, Dany is desperate for more, but can a relationship so long suppressed work outside of their own private fantasy island?

Enjoy this Smexy Excerpt from Avery Aster
Yours Truly, Taddy (The Undergrad Years #2)
by Avery Aster

No matter how hard I swam, my fears worsened. The water overwhelmed me. I could almost make out a thin sliver of land, way ahead of us, but it seemed far. I gotta ask. "Leon…"

He stopped and turned around to face me.

"Will we make Eden before dark?"

"No—"

"What are we gonna do?"

"The moonlight can guide us," Leon replied in all seriousness. However to me, he sounded almost romantic. I had to put my mind into some state of fantasy. Otherwise I'd go nuts with the reality of what we were doing: swimming for our life. "Need a break?"

"Please." I wasn't as tired as I thought I'd be. If anything, my fears supercharged me.

He swam over, put his arms around me, and asked, "Thirsty?"

"Ah-huh, and hungry." Let's not forget horny.

"Me too." Leon brushed up me. I could've sworn I felt— "Sorry," he muttered in a low voice.

"I'm not."

"What?"

"You're fine." Heck, you're more than fine. Take me. Right here. Right now.

His nose touched mine. Intent and close, we stared at each other as if we each only had one eye. I wrapped my arms, and then my legs, around him. His erection pressed up against me. Lowering my right hand, I glided my thumb against the head of his dick. Ever so slowly, with each trace of my finger over his cock, Leon's devilish smile widened.

"Your body is tight. If you loosen your limbs, you might kick better."

Trembling, I slipped a finger into the well of my cunt. I couldn't help myself, Leon was right, every muscle in my body tensed. Not from the swim, but from being in his arms. He made me nervous and excited. Until meeting Leon this week, I'd never felt these urges as strongly as I did now. I held on to his shoulders, kissing him all over again.

"Maybe this will help you relax." His hands, controlled and focused, found mine.

"Leon," I whispered under my breath, unsure if we should.

"Let me touch you." Kissing me, he pressed his fingers up against my g-spot. He knew exactly where to go. Even in the water, Leon hit it like a switch. Jesus!

Lip-to-lip, I whimpered into his mouth, moaning, calling out to him, "I want you." A tingly sensation overcame the lower part of my body. "Oh, I'm going to—"

"Come for me, Mon chére."He spoke as if in my daydream.

Just a little, right there, in the water, I came. Pulling him into me, I wasn't going to stop. We didn't have any condoms and I didn't care. "Fuck me. I want you inside of me." I needed him. I tightened my legs around his torso.

Forget the fact that we weren't an item, let alone floating in the middle of the Atlantic Ocean, I never thought my first time would be casual.

Regardless of the formalities, being with Leon Lartique, right this very second, sharing my body with him, suddenly felt like the most meaningful thing I'd ever done. The importance of this meant more to me than graduating from Avon Porter, getting into college, or making my own money. This, right here, what we were sharing, was the truest expression of oneself.

My brain had been awake for years, in recent times so had my heart, but not until today had I thought much about my soul, about life and death. Leon touched my soul.

Today could be my last day alive. I refused to go with regrets.

"Mon chére, I've never…had unsafe sex before."

"Ha! I've never had any kind of sex before. So skin-to-skin will be new for me too."

The tip of his dick slid inside me. Welcoming him, I took more. My muscles contracted tight around him. "Ahhh," I moaned, watching his face.

He found his groove in the water.

"Am I hurting you?" He pulled out, almost all the way.

"Amazing—keep going." To show my comfort, I fell back, floating in the water.

Weightlessness surrounded us.

In long, slow strokes, he fucked me. The sunset cast shadows across his face. His skin was illuminated with amber hues of paradise. Leon spoke to me in French, caressing my breasts, saying beautiful things to me that sounded lyrical and poetic.

For a minute, I closed my eyes, taking all of this in. Hypnotic! My senses felt intoxicated in a newfound euphoria. My hair floated around me as if petals in the wind.

The water's level rose up past my ears, over my eyelashes. Hands at my sides, they seemed unattached to the rest of me.

Leon's grip at my torso tightened. His penetration taught. Hips pulsating faster, he was going to come. So was I. Again.

Inhaling deeply through my nose, he impaled me. Just a small oval of air at the surface circled over my face. It felt cool. The rest of me was submerged into the sea with ecstasy.

A noise, faint at first, sent a humming sensation through the water. Leon's orgasm brought new meaning to…feeling the earth shake. Holy shit!

Suddenly Leon pulled me against him. I thought he was going to growl naughtiness in my ear, but instead he shouted, "Aeroplane!"

~ End of Excerpt ~

Connect with Avery Aster:
Newsletter http://eepurl.com/CQ665
Facebook http://www.FaceBook.com/AveryAster
Twitter http://www.Twitter.com/AveryAster
Goodreads http://www.Goodreads.com/AveryAster
Pinterest http://www.Pinterest.com/AveryAster
Instagram http://www.Instagram.com/AveryAster
Tumblr http://www.AveryAster.Tumblr.com/
Website: http://www.AveryAster.com

Another Smexy excerpt from Adriana Hunter
Escape From Reality
Adriana Hunter

He bent his head, his lips moving along her collarbone, dipping lower, sliding along the edge of her gown for a moment, then kissing the valley between her breasts. His hand rose, cupping one breast, kneading her flesh with firm fingers. Leila gasped with pleasure as he slid his thumb across her nipple. The exquisite sensation as it drew up hard changed her gasp to a low moan. There seemed to be a direct line between his circling thumb and a very specific spot deep between her hips.

She made a small noise as his thumb stopped its erotic circle around her hardened nipple and she heard an answering chuckle, low and deep. His lips moved from her skin, his breath hot through the satin.

Leila cried out as he slowly licked her nipple and she clutched the sheets, not out of tension, but in ecstasy. At the touch of his wet tongue over the satin, the friction of the material against her sensitive skin, she arched against him, her hips rising from the bed.

The wet satin molded to her as he repeatedly licked her nipple, occasionally nuzzling his cheek against her breast. Her body moved on its own, hips undulating from side to side, her back arching against his mouth. When he slowly pulled the wet satin aside and blew across her damp skin, she cried out, her nipple puckering even more, a wash of goose bumps prickling her skin.

He pulled her breast into his mouth, sucking hard, almost greedily. Leila felt his body moving in time with hers, the hip resting against hers pressing against her as she rose.

His hand moved to her other breast, pulling back the gown, fondling her briefly before he moved to suck that breast.

Leila's body was suffused with a liquid heat, coursing through her, pooling deep inside her. Her fingers found their way back to his hair, winding through the thick strands.

Finally he looked up at her, his eyes meeting hers. He sat up, took her hands, and pulled her upright.

"This comes off." His voice was rough with passion and he tugged impatiently on the gown. Leila rose to her knees and he helped her slide the gown over her head. Before she could lie back, he wrapped his arms around her, burying his face between her breasts, turning his head, kissing her softly. He held her and she held his head gently to her body.

After a moment, he let her go and she sat back, hands reaching for his shirt. He watched her in the dim light as she undid the buttons with trembling fingers. As she reached the last button, her hand brushed across his lap, across the bulge of his erection. Leila hesitated, resting her hand on him, feeling the heat and hardness his jeans concealed. He drew in a sharp breath, grabbing her hand.

"Lie back." He stood, removing his shirt, dropping it to the floor as she lay back on the sheets.

His eyes never left hers as he undid the button and zipper on his jeans. Leila tried to hold his gaze, but her eyes slid over his chest, past the flat stomach and taut navel, then lower as he began tugging his jeans over his narrow hips. This was exactly what she'd described in her assignment, every detail—almost every detail. He was perfect.

As his jeans slid lower, the dark line of hair she'd written about appeared, the line that extended below his navel, growing thicker as he lowered his jeans. Leila's breathing was shallow and fast, practically panting, eyes widening in anticipation. He tugged the jeans a fraction of an inch lower and Leila's breath stopped. Slowly, he leaned over Leila, rested a hand beside her, and blew out the candle.

For a fraction of an instant, there was silence and then Leila cried out in frustration. He laughed from somewhere nearby, and she heard the sound of his jeans hitting the floor. The mattress dipped with his weight and she felt the heat of his body a moment before his hand slid across her stomach. He leaned close and she drew in his scent, rich and spicy, deeply masculine.

There was no moonlight, and for an instant Leila cursed the darkness. But the hand on her stomach moved lower and she forgot about what he looked like, only able to focus on where his hand was going.

Fingers slid between her legs as his mouth found hers. He claimed her again with a powerful kiss, and she instinctively wound her arms around his neck, holding him close. Her legs moved on their own accord, hips rising, thighs falling open at his touch.

And then his touch moved lower, further, feather-light strokes deepening as his kiss deepened, fingers probing deeper as his tongue took possession of her mouth. Her moans were muffled against his lips, his throaty growl against hers.

He shifted his weight, one long leg moving over the top of hers. His hip pressed against her body and she felt his erection, hard and hot, rubbing against her skin. But that wasn't enough contact. She craved more, much more. Wiggling beneath him, she pulled and guided him until he rested between her legs, his hips pinning her to the mattress.

Lifting his head, he broke their kiss. She felt his breath against her cheek, his open mouth brushing against her neck. He shifted his weight again and she drew her legs up his body, over the hard muscles of his thighs.

He brushed against her, hotter than she could have imagined, and his hips shifted slightly, the muscles of his thighs tensing beneath her legs as he braced himself. Leila moved her legs further up his body, bringing her hips up to meet him, opening herself to him.

There was a long moment where he held himself, poised, just touching her, moving slowly, lightly, teasing her with a hint of what was to come. She bit her lip, aching to feel him inside her, the anticipation almost overwhelming. With one movement, she knew, he'd be there, filling her completely, totally. All she needed to do was wait. Waiting was agony, but a delicious agony nonetheless.

He lifted his head and she wished for light, to see the look on his face, the passion in his eyes, the passion that matched what raced through her own body. His hips flexed as he pulled back slowly, just a little, enough to let her know he was ready. And she was more than ready for him.

Then he was there, thrusting into her, slowly, seemingly forever. Leila let out a long, low moan as he drove himself forward, her hips rolling upward, her body accepting everything he had to give her.

Finally he stopped, exhaling against her neck, holding himself inside her for a moment. Raising his head, he braced his forearms on either side of her, his fingers playing over her face, finally coming to rest in her hair, tangling themselves in the long strands. His breath moved across her forehead, and then his lips pressed against her skin.

Her hands skated over the hot skin of his back, playing over broad shoulders, down the ridge of his spine, lower, to the small of his back, and then up the sharp slope of his buttocks. She dug her fingers into firm flesh and as if spurred on by her touch, she felt the muscles beneath her hands clench, his hips driving forward even further, as impossible as that seemed.

And then he was moving, hard and fast, Leila

matching him stroke for stroke, as if all the anticipation and pent up longing had been released. He buried his face in her neck, his breath rasping harshly against her skin.

Leila tipped her head back, sounds she never realized she could make coming from her parted lips as every thrust drove her toward some unimagined plane of pleasure. Every inch of her body was alive like it had never been before. The core of her, where he lay claim to her, where they were joined, felt like a molten pool.

She lost track of time, focusing only on the movements of their bodies. At some point he slid a hand beneath her ass, fingers digging into her flesh, lifting her, his body flexing and twisting, as if there were some way he could consume more of her, or she more of him.

His sounds had deepened, moans becoming growls, growing louder, more urgent. Leila's arms were flung wide now, fingers twisting in the sheets, her body speeding toward what could only be oblivion.

He drew back from her, his chest rising from hers, and her body instantly arched upward, taking on a life of its own as his hips drove into her at a relentless pace. Something deep and powerful welled up inside her and she writhed beneath him, head thrashing from side to side. The world went soundless for a moment and then she heard herself, from a distance, then louder, clear, cry after cry as her body shuddered and twisted in his grasp. Finally the tremors slowed and she drew a shaky breath.

His arms were still wrapped around her, holding her loosely, and he thrust slowly, but not as deeply. She relaxed in his arms, letting his momentum carry her for a moment.

Gradually his thrusts became shaper, harder, more aggressive, each one accompanied by a deep grunt. Leila drew her legs higher along his body, wrapping them around his waist. Her movements triggered something in him and his arms tightened around her again, his body wrapping around hers.

With a sudden powerful thrust, he sank himself deeply, completely, holding himself still inside her. Every muscle in his body was taut, his arms like iron bands around her. She held her breath, not wanting to break his concentration, waiting for him, for what she felt certain would be his climax.

Then beneath her hands he began to move, his hips pumping hard and fast into her, each thrust accompanied by a noise so primal it sent a shiver through Leila's body. She was unprepared for the intensity of his climax, for the power of his thrusts, the animalistic noises.

Leila was swept up in his passion, in his release, her body responding to his, a fresh cascade of sensations sweeping through her. She found herself answering his cries with her own, her body alive again with ecstasy.

They held each other for a moment, arms and legs relaxing, slowly moving apart. He rolled onto his back next to her and she curled against him, hand on his chest as his arm encircled her. The soft breeze from the window played across her skin, a delicious counterpoint to the heat that spread across her body.

Leila had never felt so complete. Not just happy, but as if for the first time, something clicked inside, some connection had been made. It went beyond the physical sensations in her body. Granted, he'd saved her life, but it went deeper than that. She'd had sex before, had even had what she'd considered making love, but there had never been this connection with those men, even men she thought she'd been in love with. And yet this man was a stranger.

Leila was content, drifting into sleep, her head on his shoulder. Almost asleep, she roused herself to ask the one question she had of the man beside her.

"You never told me your name."

He shifted on the bed, his arm pulling her close, lips brushing across her forehead.

"I can't, Leila. You haven't given me one yet."

OTHER TITLES BY CATHRYN FOX

Hands On with the CEO
Yours to Take
Torn Between Two Brothers
Spring Fling
His Obsession Next Door
Flirty in Whispering Cover
Hold Me Down Hard
Holiday Spirit
Pleasure Control

**To discover even more titles by Cathryn Fox check
out her website at
www.CathrynFox.com**

About Cathryn Fox

New York Times and *USA today* Bestselling author, Cathryn is a wife, mom, sister, daughter, and friend. She loves dogs, sunny weather, anything chocolate (she never says no to a brownie) pizza and red wine. She has two teenagers who keep her busy with their never ending activities, and a husband who is convinced he can turn her into a mixed martial arts fan. Cathryn can never find balance in her life, is always trying to find time to go to the gym, can never keep up with emails, Facebook or Twitter and tries to write page-turning books that her readers will love.

Connect with Cathryn:
Newsletter: http://bit.ly/1kpQOzf
Twitter: https://twitter.com/writercatfox
Facebook:
https://www.facebook.com/AuthorCathrynFox?ref=hl
Blog: http://cathrynfox.com/blog/
Goodreads:
https://www.goodreads.com/author/show/91799.Cathryn
_Fox
Pinterest http://www.pinterest.com/catkalen/

CHAPTER ONE

Alexis Cassidy stood inside the grand villa overlooking the breathtaking Mediterranean Sea and tried to keep her jaw from dropping. She hadn't flown halfway across the country, to babysit for some rich CEO in Athens, only to come across looking like a corn-fed Iowa farm girl—one whose idea of luxurious living involved late night pizza delivery. And to think this beautiful seaside mansion was merely her employer's summer home. Heck, maybe she should forget about finishing her English degree and get involved in the software industry instead.

"Alexis," Mr. Georgiou greeted, a dazzling smile on his boyish face as he stepped farther into the airy entranceway.

"Mr. Georgiou," she responded in return, working to keep an air of professionalism about her, a difficult task considering the sudden jolt of sexual awareness turning her scholarly brain to mush. Chatting with her new employer and his four-year-old daughter over Skype was one thing, but seeing her new boss in the flesh was quite another. Not only was he smoking hot, he had an air of badness about him. Everything from his dark, sexy eyes, the rebellious length of his hair, to the confident way he moved had lust exploding inside her. As her body registered every delicious inch of him—and from the bulge in his jeans, he clearly had many delicious inches—she blew a long strand of hair off her face and shifted her purse to conceal the telltale hardening of her nipples.

The soles of his shoes tapped on the marble floor as he closed the distance between them and perfect white teeth flashed against his rich olive complexion when he said, "Welcome to our summer home."

Alexis extended her arm for a shake, but Mr. Georgiou put his hands on her shoulders and kissed her on both cheeks, one of the many Greek customs she'd read about before beginning her overseas journey. He crowded her as his mouth brushed one cheek and then the other, his warm minty breath washing over her face in scintillating ways. Hyperaware of his closeness, she became very aware of just how young and athletic he was, very aware of the way her body reacted when he pressed against her, his soft lips so damn close to hers.

So damn close...

Behind her Mr. Georgiou's limousine driver placed her luggage on the marble tile floor. "Will that be all, sir?" he asked, and Alexis inched back, thankful for the distraction before she did something that could only embarrass them both, something like angle her head so his lips landed squarely on hers.

She turned to the driver and worked to regain her composure; pretending her boss's close proximity and feel of his lips brushing her cheeks hadn't turned her knees to rubber or warmed her in all the wrong places. Exhaling slowly, she reached for her purse to give the driver a tip.

"I've got this, Alexis," Mr. Georgiou said in a thick

Greek accent that sent little shivers skittering up her spine. He pulled out his wallet and stepped past her, the warm sandalwood scent of his skin curling her toes and teasing all her senses as it enveloped her. The muscles on his forearms bunched beneath the rolled up sleeves of his light blue dress shirt and it was all Alexis could do not to drool.

The man was a freaking Greek God!

She knew he was young and good looking when she'd Skyped with him a few weeks back, but the distorted image on her tablet didn't do the man justice. She also knew his multimillion-dollar software company had landed him and his partner on *Forbes'* "30 under 30" list. The man was smart, successful, driven.

Single.

Of course he hadn't always been single, but after losing the love of his life during the birth of their daughter four years ago, he'd become reclusive for a time, removing himself from the public's eyes. He reappeared as—according to the rag mags—one of Europe's richest, most eligible bachelors. Photos of him filled the tabloids, a different woman on his arm in every shot. Rumors of relationships were immediately shot down, the captions always reading the same: *according to a close personal friend, Mr. Georgiou and his current companion deny rumors of commitment...*

Alexis liked his way of thinking. She wasn't in the market for a full-time partner, either. Nor was she looking for love. She simply wanted a man to help her get in touch with her sexual self, and to teach her a thing or two in the bedroom. She cringed as she thought about the one and only guy she slept with at last year's football party. She was pretty sure he was simply giving the chubby girl a pity fuck, and when it was over, College Boy walked away and told his buddies she wasn't just fat, she was frigid.

The whole experience had been horrible and embarrassing. Not only had the reputation clung like a sweaty sports sock, following her around her entire first year of college, it was the last football party she'd been invited to. Which was why she planned to go on a strict diet for the next two months, learn her way around the bedroom, and return home a new woman. Then she'd show them!

Her glance moved over Mr. Georgiou, taking pleasure in the self-assured way he moved. He certainly looked like the guy who could give her what she needed, but he was her boss, which meant he was completely off limits. Still, she couldn't wait to text Melanie back home and tell her all about him.

As Mr. Georgiou spoke with his driver, Alexis stifled a yawn and waved to the little girl with the big brown eyes and thick dark hair as she ran into the foyer and latched on to her father's leg. Sophie waved back, and then Alexis put her hands over her face to play peek-a-boo. With two younger brothers, and having spent her high school years babysitting for nearly every family on her block, Alexis was used to being around kids. Which was why, when the ad for an *au pair* went up on the bulletin board outside the student employment center at her college—an *au pair* who majored in English and could help Mr. Georgiou's daughter refine her speech— she'd jumped all over it.

The benefits of taking the job were twofold. Not only did she need the money, which turned out to be a substantial sum, but rumor had it the men in Greece liked their women plump. With any luck she'd meet a hot guy during her time off from the job, gain a little more experience and learn to loosen up in the bedroom department before her upcoming sophomore year. A shiver moved through her. She never wanted to be called frigid again!

With the driver gone, her new boss turned back to her. "Alexis, it's so finally nice to meet you in person," he said, taking her right hand between his palms. "I'm sure you must be exhausted after travelling all day."

"I'm a little tired," she admitted. Actually she was exhausted. She'd gotten up at the crack of dawn, only to discover her flight had been delayed. She'd sat at the airport for hours, forcing herself to stay awake for fear of losing her luggage, and hadn't touched down in Greece until late this evening.

The sound of footsteps heralded someone's approach. She glanced past Mr. Georgiou to see an elderly gentleman enter the grand entranceway and collect her luggage. Dressed in formal wear, she took him to be the butler. Even though everything about the place, from the limo driver to the butler, seemed so formal, Mr. Georgiou himself appeared a little more laid back, a little easier going.

After Mr. Georgiou introduced her to the tall man with the graying hair he looked at her and said, "Damien has your room all ready for you. I'm sure you'll like it. It has one of the best views in the house." When she gave him a thankful smile, his handsome face softened, making him look even more boyish, like he could be any one of the guys sitting next to her in lecture hall. "You should try to get some sleep. Tomorrow we can go over the details of your duties."

"Okay," she agreed when Damien moved to the foot of the grand staircase.

Mr. Georgiou's voice dropped an octave, and sounded highly suggestive when he said, "And Alexis, if you need anything, anything at all, don't hesitate to ask."

Anything at all…

Alexis swallowed, heat zinging through her blood as she considered the provocative edge to his voice. When she stole another glance at him, he gave her a polite smile, nothing on his attractive face to suggest he'd been hinting at something more intimate.

She shook her head to clear it, sure her jet-lagged mind was simply playing tricks on her.

His hand cut through the air. "Our home is your home and we want you to be comfortable here."

"Thank you," she said, relaxing as she once again took in the opulence of the place.

"But before you go…" Mr. Georgiou put his hands on his daughter's shoulders and moved her in front of him. "I'd like you to meet Sophie. Sophie, you remember Skyping with Alexis don't you?"

Sophie nodded, peeking up at Alexis shyly as she curled her ponytail around her finger.

"Hi, Sophie," Alexis said, then crinkled her nose, and looked up the huge staircase. Hoping to put the child at ease by enlisting her help and assigning her responsibilities, she said, "I'm glad you're here to help me out and show me around. Otherwise I might get lost in this place."

Sophie stopped playing with her hair, and stood a little taller, clearly liking the idea of being in charge. "I won't let you get lost," she said, a childish confidence to her voice.

"I knew I could count on you." She held her hand out to the little girl, and nodded toward the wide staircase. "Do you think maybe you can help me find my room?" From her previous exchanges with Mr. Georgiou, she knew how much the girl loved the ocean, so she added, "If I get lost in the hall for days, I'll never be able to take you to the beach tomorrow."

Sophie giggled and when she stepped forward and accepted Alexis's hand, Mr. Georgiou smiled. "I can already see Sophie is in good hands."

Her glance went to his chin, to where he was scrubbing his palm over his five o'clock shadow.

Speaking of good hands…

Shaking off a shiver, she let Sophie lead her to the stairs, but stopped when Mr. Georgiou said, "Oh, and Alexis, one more thing." She turned and when dark, sexy eyes locked on hers, heat moved through her body. She swallowed the little rush bubbling in her throat and opened her mouth to speak, but before she could find her words, he said, "Call me Nikko."

"Okay," she managed to push out. "I'll see you in the morning, Nikko." She turned her attention to the massive staircase, hoping her knees wouldn't fail her as she climbed. She gripped the handrail, and held tight as she made her way up.

She chattered with Sophie as the little girl showed her to her lavish room. Once Damien delivered her luggage, he shooed Sophie out so Alexis could have some privacy while getting settled in. After the two disappeared, she spread her arms wide and couldn't keep the smile from her face. She took it the king-sized mattress, pretty floral bedding, gorgeous furniture and the *en suite* bathroom that was hers and hers alone. A little squeal sounded in her throat as she reveled in her good fortune. She grabbed her phone from her bag, punched in Melanie's number and walked to the elaborate, floor-to-ceiling window with a spectacular view of the moonlit ocean. She pushed back the sheer curtain, released the latch on the window to push them open, and breathed in the salty sea air. A warm breeze rushed inside and ruffled her lacy curtains.

"Oh. My. God," she whispered when she spotted the infinity pool overlooking the ocean. She could just imagine herself lounging beside that pool, sipping a fruity drink and staring out at the view.

"Oh. My. God. What?" Melanie asked, concern in her voice.

She shrieked when she heard her friend. "Mel, you

wouldn't believe this place."

"Oh Jesus, you scared the living shit out of me," she scolded. Then she gave a loud sigh and said, "I knew it would be awesome."

"Awesome doesn't even begin to describe it."

"Tell me everything," Mel demanded, and Alexis could just picture her friend throwing herself on her bed, pissed off that she was stuck at home working the corn fields instead of taking her own *au pair* job like she wanted. "If I can't be there, then you at least have to let me live vicariously through you. So now tell me everything, and don't leave out a single detail."

Alexis shot a glance toward her closed door and lowered her voice. "Nikko is unbelievably gorgeous."

"Nikko," she sighed again. "Even his name is hot."

"Everything about him is hot."

"Wait, you're on a first name basis with him?" Mel asked.

"He insisted."

"Umm," Mel purred. "Sounds like a man who likes being in control. I wonder what else you'd do if he insisted."

Alexis laughed. "He's my boss and I want to keep this job," she said, even though she secretly wondered that herself.

"He might be your boss but not only is he young, gorgeous and a notorious playboy; he's fucking rich, Alex. Rich!"

Exactly, which was why he had numerous waif-like models throwing themselves at him and wouldn't give a plump farmer's daughter a second glance. Not that she would ever try to seduce her boss, or act on the delicious things he made her feel, but it still didn't stop her from thinking about it.

Deciding to redirect the conversation, Alexis pulled her curtain back, taking in all the other mansions dotting the mountain. "Nikko was right, the view is breathtak…" Her voice trailed off, her tongue thickening at the unexpected vision before her, a vision more beautiful than the cerulean waters lapping against the sandy shoreline far below her window.

"Hello? Alex, are you still there?"

"Oh my God."

"Now what!"

"I just saw my neighbor." Patio lanterns illuminated the grounds next door, giving sufficient light for her to see the man in the scant bathing suit as he climbed onto the diving board. Her glance moved over him, trailing down the firm ridges of his abdomen, to follow the sexy line of hair that disappeared into the material that did little to hide the huge bulge her fingers suddenly itched to explore. A wheezing sound escaped her lips. Alexis squinted her eyes and focused on his torso…and the area due south. Surely it was a play of the lanterns reflecting off the water that caused all those mouthwatering ridges, bulges and dips on his body? Sort of, nature's way of Photoshopping.

She heard Mel sigh. "I take it he's hot too."

"Oh yeah. He's in a Speedo and he just dove into his pool." Alex gripped the curtain and leaned out her window for a better view. When Mr. Speedo surfaced on the other end, his hand came up to smooth his hair back and his gaze lifted to her bedroom window. A small, sensual smile touched his mouth when their gazes collided beneath the moonlight. Alexis dropped the curtain and jumped back, her heart hammering against her ribcage.

"Oh, shit. He just caught me staring." She quickly threw herself on her bed, her long dark curls splaying across her pillowcase. "How frigging embarrassing. He probably thinks I'm a voyeur." She clamped her hand over her eyes at the thought, then snorted and flung it back onto her pillow. Too late for that now.

"The hell with being embarrassed. That's fucking hot! Let him know you're looking. Let him know you're interested, that you like what you see. Isn't that what you wanted—a sexy man to notice you, to give you some experience?"

"Yes, but…"

"No buts. This is it, girl. Don't you dare puss out. Go for it!"

Alex's stomach tightened as she thought about opening the curtain again, doing exactly as Mel suggested. Instead she groaned and rolled to her side.

"I'm not like you, Mel."

"Come on, Alex. One of the reasons you took this job was to sample the local cuisine."

"I know," she groaned and rubbed her hand over her stomach where butterflies took flight at the thought of Mr. Speedo pulling her into his arms and… "but he's so incredibly hot."

"So are you."

She frowned, knowing otherwise, but instead of dwelling on her full figure, she asked, What if he's married?"

"What if he's not?"

"But he's Nikko's neighbor." What if she made a move on him and he wasn't interested in more than flirting. If he told Nikko, she'd have to live with the embarrassment for the duration of her stay. On the other hand, what if she didn't act on it, and missed out on the very thing she'd come to Greece for?

"Perfect."

Alexis ran her hand along the soft bedding. "Why is that perfect?"

"Because," she began, stretching out that one word. "if you can watch him, it means he can watch you, too."

"And what exactly will he be watching?" Alexis

asked, not sure if she wanted to hear the answer.

"You, sunbathing by the pool, topless, and bending over. A lot."

Alexis laughed. "You are so bad."

"And I bet Mr. Speedo is so fucking *good*."

As a surge of heat moved through her, Alexis climbed from the bed and inched her curtain open again. She stole another peek at her young, well-built neighbor as he lounged against the side of the pool, his arms braced on the ledge, showing off a hard body that was clearly made for sex.

Alexis gulped when he glanced her way again.

"Oh shit, he's looking at me," she whispered into the phone, her pulse leaping like mad.

"Good, now give him something to look at," Mel said.

He gave her a lopsided panty melting smile and crooked his finger.

"Oh. My. God. He's inviting me to come down."

Her friend squealed. "Jesus, Alex. Go for it."

Alexis's body flushed hotly as she pictured herself accepting his invitation, going down there in the sexy thong bathing suit Mel insisted she buy, and joining her hot neighbor in the pool like it was the most natural thing in the world for her to do.

She wet her bottom lip and asked in a low voice, "You really think I could seduce him?"

"Yes, girlfriend, I know you can seduce him. So get down there and do it!"

CHAPTER TWO

The sound of little feet running in the hall pulled Alexis awake. She stretched out on her huge bed, and as memories of last night came back to her, she felt a little rush in her stomach. God the things Mr. Speedo did to her, using his hands, his fingers, his magnificent tongue—things she'd only ever heard other girls bragging about, but had yet to experience herself.

Too bad it had only been in her dreams.

She gave a wistful sigh and rolled to her side, wondering what it would feel like to have his mouth on her skin, her breasts, between her legs, while she in turn explored his body, taking his cock into her hands, between her lips, deep into her body.

Last night she'd been too chicken shit to accept Mr. Speedo's invitation, but if she wanted to have sex, good sex, and learn her way around a man's body, she was going to have to take Mel's advice, step out of her comfort zone and go for it.

As she thought about seducing her neighbor, she climbed from the bed and stole a peek out her window. Sunlight glittered on the pool below, but her sexy neighbor was nowhere to be found. She glanced at her clock, rising a bit later than she intended. She'd forgotten to set her clock last night, her thoughts too preoccupied with Mr. Speedo.

Hurrying into the bathroom, she quickly showered, and pulled on a prim sundress that hid her curves, wanting to look the part of an *au pair* as she received her instructions from Nikko.

After getting ready she rushed down the stairs and wandered through the estate until she heard Nikko's deep voice teasing his daughter. She stepped through French doors leading outside and found her boss and his little girl eating pancakes at a table overlooking the ocean. She breathed in the salty air, and still couldn't believe she was going to be child sitting for a Greek God, who had an Adonis for a neighbor, in beautiful Athens for two whole months. This summer was going to be way more interesting than she'd ever anticipated.

"Good morning," she said, when Sophie and Nikko glanced her way.

Around a mouth full of pancake, Sophie greeted her in her native tongue. Nikko gave his daughter a quick lesson on manners, and reminded her to use her English with her *au pair*, then he turned to Alexis. His lips parted in a sexy grin, making him appear even more boyish and incredibly adorable.

"Good morning, Alexis." The greeting rolled off his tongue in that knee-weakening accent as he stood to pull a chair out for her. Unaccustomed to such chivalry, his actions caught Alexis by surprise, and she wondered if all Greek men were this courteous. It also made her wonder if they would be as thoughtful in the bedroom. Would they see to their woman's needs first, or simply take what they wanted. Would they be discrete afterward, or brag to a friend about the pity fuck for the fat chick the night before?

"How was your room?" he asked pulling her thoughts back.

"It's perfect," she said, breathing in his enticing sandalwood scent as she stepped up to the chair he held out for her.

"And the view?"

Her heart leapt at the mention of her view, but surely he couldn't know what she'd been admiring from her bedroom window. "Amazing," she said, doing her best to sound casual.

"Glad to hear it. So you slept well?" His warm breath ruffled the fine hairs on the back of her neck as his sexy accent sent shivers skittering down her spine.

She worked to concentrate on the question, rather than the deep, sensuous timber of the voice asking it. "Very well," she managed to get out, struggling to stay focused on the conversation as she lowered herself into the padded deck chair. "And I didn't mean to sleep in," she said. She waved her hand toward the sea. "Must be all this fresh ocean air."

"No need to apologize. I gave instruction for you not to be woken. I wanted to make sure you got the rest you needed."

Her heart warmed. Not only was she attracted to his looks, she was attracted to his thoughtfulness. He really was different from the guys back home. In need of a distraction, before she gave any more thought to how much she liked Nikko, she turned to Sophie, who was shoving a huge bite of blueberry pancake into her mouth. She pointed to her plate. "Those look yummy."

"Maria will make you a stack," Nikko said, taking his seat beside her.

Remembering her strict diet, she shook her head. "No, I'll just have fruit."

Nikko gave her an odd look, then opened his mouth like he was about to say something. But when a slender woman with beautiful silver hair came out on the deck he reached for his coffee, and gestured with a nod. "Maria this is Alexis, Sophie's new sitter."

Maria nodded then turned to Alexis. "Welcome, Alexis," she said. "How about a nice cup of coffee to get your morning started?"

"Yes, please," Alexis said, thinking the woman had read her mind.

Maria quickly returned with coffee and Alexis accepted the cup, skipping the rich cream and sugar she loved so dearly. As she sipped, Nikko filled her in on Sophie schedule. "When she naps in the afternoon, you're free to enjoy the pool. There's a monitor in place so you'll hear her when she wakes. Your evenings are your own, and the city has lots to offer. I'm sure you must be interested in the nightlife, and getting out to a meet few of the locals."

Her glance drifted to Mr. Speedo's estate, which was visible from Nikko's deck. Her thoughts went back to her conversation with Mel. She took a brief moment to envision herself in the pool wearing the miniscule bikini that left little to the imagination. She bit back a breathy moan, wondering if she had the nerve to wear it, to bend over and expose her plump backside to her neighbor. What if her curvy body turned him off?

What if it didn't?

She rolled her tongue around a suddenly dry mouth and shifted in her seat to hide her body's reactions, but there was nothing she could do to stop her cheeks from warming. With her pale skin she could only imagine the flush would raise her boss's curiosity.

He pushed back in his chair. "Are you okay, Alexis?"

She swallowed, jerked her gaze back to her coffee, and fanned herself. "I'm uh…not used to this warm weather," she explained.

"I see." Nikko took a long drink from his mug, and

angled his head to see what she'd been staring at. When he looked back at her, his eyes darkened, and his gaze moved over her face. "I'm sure you'll get used to the…heat…around here quickly enough."

Everything in the slow way he said *heat* had her skin coming alive, because suddenly she had the sneaking suspicion that he wasn't talking about the weather at all, and that he knew she had the hots for his neighbor. And maybe even for him.

"I'm sure I will," she said when Maria came with a plate of fruit for her.

As she nibbled, Nikko continued to explain Sophie's schedule, then put his napkin on the table and said, "I'd love to spend more time with you two lovely ladies, but it's time for me to get to work."

Sophie giggled, showcasing blueberry-stained teeth when she said, "Bye, Papa."

He dropped a kiss onto Sophie's head, then gave Alexis a wink. "You be a good girl today, Sophie and be sure Alexis doesn't get lost this morning on the way to the beach. I'll see you before your nap."

"You'll be stopping back?" Alexis asked.

"I actually work from home during the summer, so I can spend more time with Sophie." He stood and pointed to a corner room on the ground floor. As Alexis took in the huge window overlooking the pool, he said, "That's my office. If you need anything at all, my door is always open."

Alexis gulped air, as she ran through Melanie's scandalous plan. If she sunbathed in the nude, Nikko's neighbor wouldn't be the only one to see her. Nikko would have a front row seat as well! A strange, scintillating shiver moved through her as she imagined that scenario. The thought of those dark eyes on her as she untied her top, peeled it off and bared her breasts to the sun. Or better yet, two pairs of eyes…heat curled low in her belly and settled between her legs, dampening her panties.

"I'll see you both later."

Alexis mumbled good bye as Nikko sauntered away, and she couldn't help but notice how nicely he filled out his white dress shirt and tan colored pants. The computer guys she knew were lanky and wore sweats, Nikko appeared to take extra care with his appearance, and she liked that about him.

When he rounded the corner, Alexis turned her attention to Sophie, shaking off the salacious things Nikko made her feel. He was her boss, and he was off limits, she reminded herself.

"So what do you say, should we hit the beach?" she asked the little girl.

"Beach!" Sophie squealed.

"Maybe we can build a sand castle."

"Mermaid," she countered, and climbed down from the chair.

"Okay, you go get your bathing suit, and I'll gather up some beach towels and buckets." Alexis followed Sophie into the kitchen and found Maria at the counter, a beach bag in hand.

"You're all set. Nikko told me you two would probably be hitting the beach this morning, and gave me instructions on what to pack." Her glance moved over Alexis's pale skin and she crinkled her nose. "Just be sure to use lots of lotion. Sophie will need some too."

Alexis took the beach bag and looked inside to find a bottle of SPF 50. She grinned, surprised that Nikko had anticipated her needs and seen to it that they were taken care of. That last thought had her thinking of sex and warmth spread over her skin.

"I'll guess I'll grab my suit then." She darted up the stairs behind Sophie, who was singing the theme song to *The Little Mermaid.*

Once inside her bedroom, Alexis rifled through her suitcase. Normally she wore a one piece that hid more of her curves than they revealed, but here, well, most didn't wear a suit at all and a one piece would make her stand out like a tourist. Since she wanted to blend in with the local crowd, and the fact that Mel had hidden her old suit, it was either a two-piece or nothing at all. She looked over the one Mel had picked out for her and knew it was too risqué to wear to the beach with Sophie. She'd save that one for later, for when she was at the pool alone. Bending over. A lot.

Oh gawd.

She stripped out of her dress and pulled on the modest yellow bikini she had brought along to wear in mixed company. After wrestling her big breasts into cups that seemed to have grown smaller, studied herself in the mirror. Even though her nanny suit was modest, it still exposed more skin than she was comfortable with. Feeling unsure, she grabbed her phone, took a selfie and sent it to Mel.

Yes or no?

A minute later her friend responded.

Hell yes, you look gorgeous.

She smiled. Despite the fact that her body image issues ran deep, Mel still always found a way to make her feel better about herself. When a soft tap sounded on her door, she exhaled slowly, and even though she felt self-conscious exposing so much of her body, she decided to go for it.

She grabbed her bathing suit cover up, and opened her door to find a very cute Sophie in a pink bikini. "You look very pretty," Alexis said.

"You're pretty too," the little girl said, poking her finger into the swell of Alexis's tummy, making her feel more like the Pillsbury Doughboy than a sexy sophomore hell bent on gaining more experience in the bedroom.

Instead of going straight to the beach, they went in to town where she got a walking tour from a very knowledgeable four-year-old. Thirty minutes later they made their way to the ocean. At this early hour they practically had the whole beach to themselves. She bent forward to lay out their towels, and when she stood and took off her cover-up, she had to adjust her top to keep her breasts restrained.

Sophie had already shed her beach jacket and was digging into the sand by the time Alexis got the lotion out. "Come here, kiddo."

She found an elastic band in the beach bag and tied Sophie's dark hair into a ponytail, then she went up on her knees, and squirted lotion onto the child's olive skin. "You are such a pretty girl," she said as she rubbed it in, and Sophie beamed in response.

"She's not the only one."

The sound of a man's voice coming from behind had her spinning around.

Her heart jumped into her throat when she spotted Mr. Speedo hovering close. "Oh, I…" she said, unable to get any words out. "I didn't hear…"

Wait…did he just say she was pretty too?

"Dimi," Sophie squealed.

"Hey, short stuff," he said, and tugged on her ponytail.

"You two know each other?" Alexis asked before she could think better of it. Of course they knew each other, they were neighbors, after all. Feeling nervous and anxious as Mr. Speedo stood over her, the impressive bulge in his bathing suit merely inches from her salivating mouth, she looked for something to do. She poured a generous amount of lotion on her arm and began to lather it in with much more force than necessary.

He winked at Sophie. "Sophie is my very best friend. Aren't you, Sophie?"

Sophie giggled and he stepped up to her and grabbed the bucket. "Why don't you go get some water for the sand castle?"

"Sand mermaid," she corrected and happily trotted off toward the water.

Dark eyes met hers and his voice dropped an octave when he said, "You must be Sophie's new nanny."

Keeping one eye on Sophie as she filled the bucket, Alexis nodded, and chafed her arms harder, trying to ignore the way his scent—an enticing mixture of sun, sand and sex—aroused all her senses.

"Alexis," she said, her dry throat cracking.

"I'm Dimitri."

She glanced at his hand, and his empty ring finger reminded her of her conversation with Melanie. He might be single, but now that she'd gotten a look at him, a real good look at him, she was having some doubts about seducing him. Everything from his athletic, sun-kissed body, the wild look about him to the sexy tattoo on his arm warned he was out of her league and wouldn't be interested in a plump, inexperienced farm girl like her. He probably only invited her over last night to be polite to his neighbor, not because he wanted her. Or maybe she'd misinterpreted his gesture and he was simply shooing a bug away. Cripes, she had to be out of her mind for even entertaining the idea of seducing him.

He cocked his head, and his too long bangs fell into his eyes. "How are you enjoying Athens so far?"

She looked out over the water and exhaled slowly. "It's beautiful here."

"Yes, the view is beautiful, breathtaking really," he said, but when Alexis turned back to him, he wasn't looking at the ocean, he was looking at her.

He was looking at her!

Was it possible? Could he *be* interested?

After rubbing the lotion onto her arms and legs, she accidently squirted over half the bottle on her shoulders. Shit! Maybe she could scoop some of it off before he noticed. Twisting around, she slid her fingers into the glob of lotion and began to rub hastily.

He took the bottle from her and dropped down behind her, his knees bracketing her hips. "Here let me help."

Fearing she'd melt like a Popsicle if he touched her, she said, "You don't have…"

"But you're doing it wrong, Alexis," he murmured softly into her ear, the heat in his voice licking over her thighs and eliciting a shiver from deep within. The second his big warm hands touched her skin, a tremble moved through her, and a whimper bubbled up from the depths of her throat.

"A little goes a long way," he explained, his touch shockingly intimate. "And you need to rub slowly, like this." Deft palms moved over her shoulders and down her back, skating seductively over her flesh as he worked the lotion in. "When you're under the Mediterranean sun, you have to take care to coat every inch, even the spots you don't think need it. Usually those hidden spots are the ones that need it the most."

As she thought about all her hidden spots and his fingers sliding over them, she damn near swallowed her tongue.

"Like here for instance." The soft pad of his thumb slipped under the knot holding her top together, where he rubbed with careful precision. The non-sexual gesture felt so—sexual. As he lightly massaged the lotion into her flesh, Alexis couldn't help but wonder how his fingers would feel on another part of her body. Each brush of his fingers over her skin echoed along her sex and she wiggled slightly, struggling to calm the ache between her legs.

She moistened her lips, searching for something to say. But her body was too hot, her pussy to needy, making coherent speech near impossible.

"There you go," he murmured, and she was sure she was going to climax from the sound of his voice alone. He gestured toward the water. "Just remember to reapply if you get wet."

Ah, Jesus, I'm already wet.

When Sophie came back carrying a bucket of water, he recapped the bottle, tossed it beside her and stood. He stole a glance at his watch. "I'll see you later, Sophie."

"Bye," she mumbled absently as she reached for her shovel.

His muscles bunched as he shifted his stance, moving directly in front of Alexis. His glance slid over her before moving back to her face. He paused for a moment, then said, "Don't make any plans for tonight."

She swallowed. Hard. "What?" she asked, trying not to ogle his body. "Why?"

His smile stretched wickedly. "I'm having a pool party." He shaded the sun from his eyes and said, "You should come."

"I should?"

As if he could read her innermost thoughts he said, "It's a good chance to meet a few of the locals, and see what the night life is like around here." He gave a knowing smile and said, "Otherwise it will be an awfully long summer stuck in that room of yours every night, don't you think?"

"It's not so bad." She shrugged, and suddenly, feeling very brave and flirtatious, she added, "The view is rather nice."

With that he laughed out loud, and she couldn't help but grin. Jesus, what the hell had come over her? She never flirted with a guy so brazenly before, and never with one as hot as Dimitri. Perhaps the sun was getting to her, or maybe the second his hands had touched her body she knew she had to know what those hands of his would feel like caressing every inch of her body, especially all the hidden parts.

"Yeah, well it was nice from where I was standing, too." A low chuckle rumbled in his throat and she expected he was a man who always got what he wanted when he added, "I expect to see you later, Alexis."

Chapter Three

Music from Dimitri's back yard drifted in through Alexis's open bedroom window and a nervous quiver moved through her. Sure she came here wanting to find a man to give her experience, but she'd never expected an Adonis like Dimitri to flirt with her, let alone invite her to his party. She looked through her wardroom again, and had pretty much decided against going, considering nothing seemed appropriate for a lavish pool party given by a very wealthy Greek Adonis, who undoubtedly had women throwing themselves at him. She sent Melanie a text.

I'm not going.

The hell you're not!

I have nothing to wear.

You have your sexy new bathing suit.

I have nothing to wear over it.

It's a pool party, Alex. You don't need to wear anything over it. Get over there and show off that sexy body of yours.

Alex stole a glance out her window. She took in the posh crowd, and their skimpy outfits as they mingled near the pool. Honestly, compared to what the other women were wearing, her barely there bathing suit looked more like a potato sack, than a skimpy bikini.

Her phone made the little "zip" sound when Melanie texted her back.

Come on, Alex. If you won't do it for you, at least do it for me. Last night I ended up drinking beer out on the back forty and doing the horizontal shake with Johnny Simpson. It wasn't my best moment.

Alexis cringed. *Ugh, what were you thinking?*

I know, right?

I guess you really do need me to do this for you.

So does that mean you'll do it?

She sat on the window ledge and gazed longing at Dimitri's pool, trying to summon the courage to don the tiny bikini dangling from her fingertips, and walk over there like attending elaborate pool parties in a sexy thong was an everyday occurrence. As she took deep breaths, Dimitri's parting words came back to her.

I expect to see you later, Alexis.

Good God, if she put on her new suit and went over there, he'd definitely be *seeing* her. Every plump inch of her, except for a couple of miniscule patches.

Her glance surfed through the crowd a second time and when it landed on Dimitri, her heart gave a little jump. He stood at the edge of his pool, his dark head tipped toward her window. Everything in the way he was looking up at her, his grin sexy, his eyes so full of heat and promise had her breath catching.

She sent Mel another text. *He's looking at me.*

Which means he's interested, so get your ass down there, and send me pictures if you can.

Alexis drew another breath and her thoughts went back to her horrible first year at college as she powered down her phone and tossed it onto her bed. God she really wanted to go back to college a changed woman, one with a sleek, experienced body—one who was good enough to be invited to the football parties.

This is your chance, her inner voice taunted. *Just do it.*

She inched away from the window, pulled on her bikini, and avoided her mirror. One look at her overflowing cleavage and curvy hips and she'd surely tuck tail and dive under her covers. She hauled a spaghetti strap dress from her closet and slipped it on. It wasn't glamorous by any means, or suitable for Dimitri's pool party, but it would have to do the trick. Until she felt comfortable enough, she wouldn't be taking it off.

She quietly opened her bedroom door, and stole a glance around the dark hallway. With Sophie asleep, and Nikko in charge of her care after hours, she tiptoed down the hall, not wanting to disturb anyone or explain where she was going. She was pretty sure Nikko's idea of exploring the night life didn't involve getting naked with his neighbor, and if luck was with her tonight, that's exactly how the evening would end.

A few minutes later, she followed the foliage-lined path from Nikko's mansion to Dimitri's. As she glanced around, she wondered what Dimitri did for a living, considering he looked to be about the same age as Nikko and also lived in a mansion. Her heart began to pound in synch to the fast paced music as she entered his lantern-lit backyard. She stopped to take it all in, her glance moving over the crowd of partygoers, as they laughed, swam, ate and drank copious amounts of alcohol. Some of the women were dressed in bikinis and some only wearing their bottoms, but that wasn't what shocked her most. Oh no, not at all. What nearly had her scurrying back to her bedroom were the couples who were in various stages of sex, getting down and dirty on the chaise lounges, completely oblivious to everyone around them.   Then again, maybe they weren't.   Maybe they liked being watched.   Alexis shivered, recalling the way her body had reacted watching Dimitri in his pool, and how it had turned her on when she'd discovered he was watching her in return.   Before she had a chance to give it any further thought, a pretty blonde who looked only a couple years older than her stepped up to her.

"You must be Alexis."

"What?" Alexis asked, surprised the woman knew her name. "I mean, yes, I am," she added hastily, remembering her manners.

"Dimitri has been waiting for you."

"He has?" Her heart gave a little jolt. She looked through the crowd, unable to find him, but when she saw a guy working his mouth down his girl's body, she couldn't deny that it filled her with equal amounts of apprehension and excitement.

As if sensing her sudden distress, the girl gripped her hand and gave a little tug. "Come on. I think you need a drink."

She let the slender girl lead her to the bar, and even though she didn't want the extra calories from alcohol, she definitely needed a drink.

"So how do you know Dimitri?" she asked as she poured Alexis a flute of champagne and handed it over.

"Actually, I just met him." Alexis tipped the flute toward the foliage that separated the houses. "I'm here for the summer sitting for Mr. Geo...I mean Nikko."

Intrigue moved over the girl's face. "Really?"

"Yes, I was hired to watch Sophie and help with her English."

The girl looked past Alexis's shoulder to Nikko's house. "That guy is so fucking hot. Damn, what I'd do to sleep under the same roof as him." Her eyes glossed a bit when she added, "Actually, I'd like to be sleeping under *him.*" She tossed Alexis an envious look, like she was privy to something Alexis wasn't. "You're a lucky girl."

She was about to tell her Nikko was her boss and it wasn't like that, but the girl shrugged her shoulders, her ample breasts jiggling in her frilly bikini. "Anyway, I'm Zenobia, but everyone calls me Zen."

Instantly taking a liking to Zen, and hoping they could become friends over the summer, she said, "I'm Alexis," but then realized Zen already knew that. Trying to hide her nervousness, Alexis sipped her champagne and said, "This is a nice party."

Zen gave her a grin. "Dimitri's parties are legendary. We love when he comes back here for the summer."

She took a huge gulp of her champagne. "So this is his summer home?"

She nodded. "Would you like me to introduce you around, until Dimitri comes back? I think he got tied up with a business call?"

She was about to ask what Dimitri did for a living, having such an amazing summer house and all, but Zen frowned and asked, "Did you bring a bathing suit?"

Alexis put a tentative hand on the strap at the back of her neck. "It's on underneath."

"Then you might want to ditch the dress," Zen said, reaching around to pull the strings loose for her. "After all, this is a pool party," she added, a dazzling smile lighting up her pretty face.

The dress slipped to her waist, and Alexis resisted the urge to cup her breasts, barely covered by the slip of triangle, when Zen's eyes dropped to them. "Come on. I'll introduce you to my friends." Zen shook her head. "They're going to love you."

Left with no choice but to follow, Alexis glanced around as she shimmied the dress over her hips and stepped out of it. She folded it over her arm, holding it in front of her body like a shield as Zen led her through the crowd. She introduced her to so many people Alexis knew she'd never keep the names straight.

Everyone was so laid back and easy to talk to, she soon found herself having a good time, and feeling less and less conscious of her curvy body. In fact, with the way the guys were paying attention to her, she actually felt a bit sexy. Maybe it was true that the men here really did like their women curvy. She stole a glance around, looking for Dimitri, as Zen introduced her to a few more of her friends, and she was both surprised and thrilled when they suggested she join them at Club Athens over the upcoming weekend.

She sipped her champagne, accepting Zen's invite to visit the clothing boutique she owned in town, then nearly choked on her drink when a deep male voice asked from behind, "Are you having a good time, Alexis?"

Heat moved through her body, fully aware that it was Dimitri standing close. The sexy way her name rolled off his tongue, combined with his unique beachy scent filled her with a deep sense of awareness. She turned slowly, and tried to tamp down her want, but failed miserably when her glance met with dark, predatory eyes. She acknowledged the flare of desire deep between her legs and worked hard not to stare at his magnificent body. She gripped the stem of her champagne glass, resisting the urge to push his hair from his eyes as her pussy thrummed with want.

From behind her, one of the guys Zen had introduced her to said, "Hey Dimitri, you didn't tell us you had this treasure hidden next door."

"I didn't know it myself until last night," he said, without taking his eyes off her.

"So I take it you and Nikko—"

Before the guy could finish, Dimitri put his hand on the small of her back and splayed his fingers over her quivering skin. "I'll take it from here, Zen," he said, his voice gliding over her naked flesh like a rough caress. "Thanks for showing her around."

He gave a little nudge to set her into motion, and guided her to the bar where he refilled their glasses. As he poured, her glance moved over the trays of beautiful hors d'oeuvres. Despite the grumble in her stomach, she didn't dare take one of the scrumptious looking phyllo cheese triangles if she wanted to return home slim.

Dimitri slipped one into his mouth, and said, "Help yourself, Alexis."

"No thanks," she murmured.

Before she realized what was happening, Dimitri reached for another one and held it to her lips. "Open," he commanded softly. Surprised, she was about to protest, but he nudged the wedge against her mouth and she automatically obeyed. When the rich, buttery pastry settled on her tongue, the taste stimulating all her senses and filling her with euphoria, there was nothing she could do but savor the little piece of heaven.

As she chewed, Dimitri lifted his fingers to his mouth and licked them, the flick of his tongue so sensual her pussy clenched, eager for that same kind of attention.

Music filled the air and he stepped closer, the heat emanating off him practically scorching her exposed flesh. "You should never deny yourself what you want," he said with certainty, and she flushed at the intimacy in his tone.

"But I'm…" she began, then stopped herself. This man didn't know her for the chubby girl who the boys teased and dismissed.

"What you are is perfect," he murmured into her ear. "You're sexy just the way you are, Alexis," he added, giving her the sense he knew exactly what she had been about to say. He took her dress from her, placed it on a chair beside the bar, and handed her the full champagne flute. She sucked in a quick breath when he pressed his hand into her back again, to set her into motion.

As he led her to the Jacuzzi at the far end of this backyard, she replayed his words in her head.

You're sexy just the way you are.

The comment gave the boost of self-confidence Alexis needed to loosen up and enjoy the party. She breathed in the fresh night air, and took note of the people around them. She tried to appear unaffected, tried not to notice the quickening of her pulse, the ache between her legs as they moved past a couple having sex. The woman leaned over a table, legs spread, her head thrown back as her partner grasped her hips and drove into her from behind. Alexis stole a glance at Dimitri to see his reaction, and found him looking back at her, his eyes caressing her with sultry heat.

"Is everything okay?"

"Yes…I just…I'm not used to…"

"Not used to what?"

Not wanting to come off as a country bumpkin, she said, "Nothing, it's nothing."

His dark eyes moved over her face, a careful assessment. "Our culture takes some getting used to," he said softly, as if he could read her innermost thoughts.

She forced a smile, "I'm sure I'll get used to it."

"With the right guidance you will." His finger skimmed along her collar bone, and slid under the tie of her bikini top. "I'm glad to see you didn't burn today. It pleases me that you followed my directions."

"Directions?" she asked, trying not to sound breathless as he crowded her.

His hair fell into his eyes, and his grin was badass when he said, "You must have taken extra care to reapply after getting wet, being careful to massage the lotion in to all those hidden spots, like I showed you."

Hardly able to believe this gorgeous creature was

flirting with her when there were so many beautiful women around, she answered with, "You did seem to know what you were talking about. I would have been a fool not to do as I was told." Her chest heaved, fully aware of just how much guidance this man could provide, just how much she could learn from him. And how badly she wanted to be his student.

When they reached the Jacuzzi, and found a few people lounging in the hot water, chatting over a glass of champagne, Dimitri held out a chivalrous hand and helped her in. She looked at him, but there was nothing gentlemanly in the way he was staring back. God, no man had ever looked at her like that before. Her heart raced wildly as her body stirred with want. Sexual tension arced between them, making her feel edgy, out of control…desired.

As her body flushed hotly, she slid lower in the water, bubbles breaking around her as Dimitri moved closer, bringing his heat with him. Her blood pounded harder, aware at how fast things were moving. But she wanted this. Oh, how she wanted him.

"Did I hear correctly, you're going out to Club Athens this weekend?"

The dark desire in his eyes made it difficult to think. "Your friends…they invited me to go clubbing."

"You should go," he said. He took a sip of his champagne, and swiped the soft blade of his tongue over his bottom lip.

"You think so?"

He dipped his head, his mouth so close to hers she was sure he was going to kiss her. "You're here looking for an authentic Greek experience, aren't you?" he asked, and once again she suspected he could read her innermost desires.

"You know how the saying goes. When in Rome…," she said, ripples of sensual pleasure moving over her flesh as her thoughts careened in an erotic direction. "If I want a true Greek experience I must adapt myself to the customs and behave the way locals behave."

There was a teasing glint in his eye when he corrected with, "Don't you mean misbehave."

Her stomach tightened with a mixture of apprehension and excitement. She swallowed hard, gathering her bravado and said, "If that's what it takes to experience *everything.*"

"Everything?" he asked, his hungry expression letting her know they were talking about something entirely different then blending in with the locals.

His knuckles brushed hers and she shivered as his touch went right through her. Even though it was all happening so fast, and Dimitri's attention was completely overwhelming her, there was no denying he could give her what she wanted.

"Yes," she murmured and tamped down her nervousness. "Everything."

His mouth lifted in a sexy, half smile, and everything about the way he looked at her gave her confidence, made her feel sexy. "So is that really what brought you here, Alexis? The opportunity to experience *all* Greece has to offer."

Fueled by need, she decided to go for it, to let him know in no uncertain terms exactly what she was looking for. "Yes. I'm looking for a real hands-on experience."

He leaned into her, his breath warm on her face. When he shot her a suggestive look, her body responded with a tremble, despite the warmth of the water. Ignoring those around them, he put his hand on her leg. Her sex clenched almost painfully as he ran his fingers up her thighs, along the length of her side, his knuckles coming perilously close to her rock hard nipples.

He wet his mouth. "Then I suggest we get started."

Her lips parted but before she could answer, she saw the light flick on next door. When she caught the silhouette of Nikko on his deck, unease moved through her, knowing she was visible to him. Even though he'd told her that her nights and weekends were her own, she didn't want her employer to think he'd hired someone who wouldn't be a good role model for his daughter. She inched away, but oddly enough, even though she was sure she didn't have exhibition tendencies, the thoughts of Nikko watching her with Dimitri—Dimitri touching her, kissing her, burying his face between her legs to take care of the hungry spot in need of attention—filled her with a new kind of heat.

CHAPTER FOUR

Two days had passed since the pool party and Alexis hadn't seen Dimitri around since she had apologized and slipped from his Jacuzzi and hurried back to her room. As much as she wanted to stay and see where the night led, she didn't want to give Nikko any reason to send her packing. Certain she'd blown any chance with her hot neighbor, she glanced at the sexy outfit on her bed, one she'd picked up at Zen's boutique in town earlier that day. Hot as Dimitri was, maybe she'd be better off steering clear of him, all things considered, and hooking up with someone else.

When she'd stopped by the shop, Zen had insisted she come out to the club with them tonight, but after fleeing from Dimitri's party, she wasn't so sure she should. Then again, he likely didn't want to have anything more to do with the skittish American after her hasty escape and this would give her a chance to meet a few more locals.

Her phone beeped, indicating she had a text. She grabbed it from her nightstand.

Stop overthinking things and just go!

Alexis laughed. Even thousands of miles away, Mel knew what she was thinking.

Okay, okay.

And don't worry about Mr. Speedo. It's his loss, not yours.

I'm not so sure about that. You didn't see him.

I still think you should have done him. Right there in the Jacuzzi!

I told you. Nikko was watching.

Maybe that's his thing, Alex. Maybe Nikko gets off on it. Did you ever think of that?

A shimmer of excitement moved through Alexis at the thought of Dimitri touching her while Nikko watched. Her pussy quivered with anticipation. *I hardly think so.*

Yeah, well you never know.

Wanting to redirect the conversation, Alexis took a picture of the sexy top and skirt and sent it to Mel. *What do you think?*

I think the guys are going to be fighting over you.

I don't know about that, but it's gorgeous isn't it?

Yeah, so put it on and get out there and get yourself laid.

Alexis crinkled her nose, a sudden bout of apprehension moving through her. What if no one was interested? *Maybe I should just stay in.*

You know I'm dying here, right? Jesus, Alex, get dressed and get out there. I need this as much as you do!

Alexis laughed. *I'll talk to you later.*

Alex tossed her phone onto her bed, took one last look out her window in search of Dimitri, then decided the hell with it. Zen was giving her the opportunity to meet guys and she was damn well going to take it.

After dressing in the silk, cleavage-complementing top Zen had specifically picked out for her, and the short skirt that enhanced her curves, rather than hid them, she fussed with her makeup and hair. Standing before her mirror she had to admit Zen knew what she was doing. She actually felt pretty in the clothes, and with the way the guys had all admired her body at the pool party, maybe her apprehension was for nothing.

She slipped from her room, noting how unusually quiet the house was. She'd spent the day swimming with Sophie, and going over some English lessons. The little girl was pretty tuckered out at the dinner table so she assumed she was fast asleep at this late hour. She hadn't seen much of Nikko over the last couple days. He'd been out of the house buried in business meetings, and had only eaten with them a handful of times. Which was probably a good thing, because the less time she spent around him, the less she'd be thinking about what Zen had said about sleeping under him.

Or what Mel had said about him watching...

She made her way outdoors and was hit with a warm sea breeze as she walked down the cobblestone driveway and found her way to the center of town. Locals and tourists alike filled the streets, and the delicious smells of authentic Greek food wafted through the night air, making her empty stomach grumble. Music drifted from the open windows of numerous clubs, and laughter curled around her, punching up her anticipation.

As excitement built inside her, she maneuvered her way through the crowd, aware of the male attention she was drawing. Feeling a new sense of bravado, she pulled her shoulders back, accentuating her ample cleavage and put a little extra sway to her hips, letting her skirt flare around her.

She turned the corner and stepped into Club Athens. Loud music filled the packed room as she stood there suddenly feeling a little unsure as she searched for a familiar face.

"Alexis," Zen called out, and relief moved through her as her new friend waved her over.

Alexis pushed her way through the crowd, and when she reached Zen's table, Zen jumped up to hug her.

"I'm so glad you came." Zen gave her a quick once over, and whispered. "You look gorgeous." She clicked her tongue and added, "What I'd do for those curves." Before Alexis could respond, and tell her how much she'd love to have her slim shape, Zen waved her hand over the others at her table. "You remember everyone, don't you?"

She nodded, and as she sat, she wracked her brains trying to recall everyone's name. A waitress came by with drinks and finger food and everyone chatted and dug in. Alexis resolutely avoided the delicious looking fried appetizers on the platter, sipped on a cocktail and talked to Costa, who she'd come to learn, was a travel guide and offered to show her around.

Relaxing in to conversation, and feeling like a part of this accepting group of people who didn't seem to judge her based on her figure, she pushed back into her chair, prepared to enjoy the evening. But when a powerful hand came down on her shoulder, and the warm scent of beach washed over her, every nerve in her body came alive.

She didn't need to turn to know it was Dimitri. As she sat there trying to catch her breath, everyone around the table greeted him, and after exchanging pleasantries, he put his mouth close to her ear and said, "Come with me."

Working to tamp down the anxiety careening through her blood, Alexis pardoned herself from the table, noting that no one seemed surprised that Dimitri was taking her away. It was like they knew he was a man who got what he set his eyes on, and right now he had those eyes set on her! When she stood, he put his hand on the small of her back, and looked down at her with raw hunger.

Her entire body quaked. "Where are we going?" she questioned, hating how breathless she sounded.

"To finish what we started," he said with certainty as they moved through the crowd.

"What do you mean?"

He stopped in the middle of the club, and turned to her. When partygoers breezed past them, he pulled her close, her body pressed against his. "You ran away so fast the other night I didn't get to give you your first Greek, hands-on experience."

She gulped. "I left because…but I haven't seen you…I didn't think you still…"

"I've been busy, Alexis." His voice dropped, became deep, sensual, husky. "I've been swamped with meetings, but believe me, you're all I've been able to think about."

"Oh," she said.

"But work time is over." His eyes moved over her face, as his hands slid lower on her back, resting at the swell of her buttock. "And you know what that means?"

"No, what?"

His grin turned wicked, and there was a suggestive edge to his voice when he said, "It means it's time to play."

Her nipples tingled in anticipation. Her mouth opened, but words escaped her. She wondered if she looked as eager as she felt.

He dipped his head, his mouth so damn close to hers. "Isn't that what you want? Don't you want to play with me, Alexis?"

Her heart raced, pounded against her ribcage. "Yes," she answered, but then stole a nervous glance around, thinking about all the couples she'd seen having sex in public. Surely he didn't…

"Then let's play," he said.

Hoping her legs didn't fail her, she let him guide her through the throng of people, toward the end of the bar. As if understanding her worries, he pulled her into what looked like a private wine room, pressed her back to the wall, and braced his hands on either side of her head.

She looked out the archway and into the dark club. While she couldn't see into the dimness, she knew if anyone sat at the stool near the end of the bar, they'd be able to see them, but when his lips came down on hers, and he pressed his solid body into her, she could no longer think with any clarity.

He kissed her hard, his tongue sliding into her mouth to tangle with hers. After a long moment he groaned then murmured, "You're every bit as sweet as I knew you would be."

A noise crawled out of her throat and she squirmed, hardly able to believe what was happening. One minute she was sitting with her new friends, the next Dimitri had her flat against the wall. He pillaged her mouth, ran his hands down her sides, shaping her contours and stroking the outer edges of her breasts. He pressed his hips against her and a whimper crawled out of her throat when she felt the impressive length of his cock against her stomach. Her body flushed, and when she became a little lightheaded, her hands gripped his shoulders to hang on.

God, she wanted this so badly, but when he slipped a hand between her legs, she froze, her heart pounding erratically as a tremble moved through her. Air hissed from her lungs as she tried to loosen up and let nature takes its course, but her body remained stiff, a telltale sign that she was an ingénue. She bit the inside of her mouth, not wanting to come off as young and inept, but with the way she'd stiffed when he delved beneath her skirt, she was beginning to show her true colors. She was also starting to believe that College Boy was right.

Maybe she really was frigid.

Dimitri straightened and braced his hands on either side of her head again. Perceptive eyes full of heat locked on hers. "Alexis, are you okay with this?" he asked, his voice husky and raw.

"Yes." she managed to get out after a long moment.

He cocked his head. "This *is* what you want, right?"

She blinked up at him, and when her glance met with tender concern she found herself hedging the truth. "It's happening so fast."

His hair spilled over his eyes making him look so damn sexy her sex clenched. "Do you want me to slow down?"

She shook her head, her body tightening as she glanced down. "No, it's not really that."

Dimitri put a finger under her chin and lifted it until their eyes locked. "What is it?"

She nibbled her lip, and blurted out, "I might not be very good at this."

"I know," he murmured.

Surprised, her back straightened. "You do? How?"

"Sweetheart," he began, running the rough pad of his thumb over her cheek. "You have innocence written all over you."

A fine tremor rippled through her at his touch. "Then why would you want to do this? Are you taking pity on me too?"

"Pity?" He groaned and raked a hand through his hair. "Have you not looked at yourself in a mirror lately?" He shook his head. "Alexis, you're gorgeous. Do you have any idea how much I want you? Your body is so lush and inviting, all I want to do is touch you. You're all I've thought about for days."

"Really?" She sucked in a quick breath, and felt something warm and wicked blossom inside her.

"Yes, really. Why would you think otherwise?"

She shrugged, her throat tightening with emotions. "The guys back home—"

Her pressed a finger to her lip and finished her sentence. "—are assholes."

She grinned. "Yeah, I know," she agreed and took a quick moment to wonder why she even cared what they thought.

"They have no idea how to treat a beautiful, voluptuous woman like you." His lips lightly brushed hers and in a voice full of promise, he murmured, "But I do. I can give you what you want, what you need, Alexis." The roughness in his tone gave way to softness and pushed away the last of her reserve when he asked, "Isn't that why you came to me?"

"Yes," she admitted, understanding how good everyone here was at reading her needs, which had her wondering if her boss was privy to her deepest, darkest secrets too.

"Then don't think, sweetheart. Just feel."

He brushed his thumb over her mouth, and with impulse flooding her, she parted her lips and drew the rough tip into her mouth. He growled and pushed the hard ridge of his cock against her belly. Alexis sucked him in deeper, having no idea what possessed her to take his finger into her mouth in the first place. Perhaps sharing her fears with him filled her with bravado. Or perhaps it was the sexy way he looked at her that made her feel sexy, brazen.

Confident.

Either way, even though having sex at the club was risky and inappropriate, she wanted this. Here and Now. With him. And suddenly, being inappropriate felt like a good idea.

As if sensing the shift in her, he grabbed her hands and pinned them above her head, holding her captive against the wall. His burning mouth came down hard, claiming her and branding her with his heat. Delicious warmth spread over her skin as she undulated her hips against his, rubbing herself against him and giving herself over to the heat between them.

She savored the sweetness of his mouth, until he pulled away, to begin a slow path down her body. "Dimitri," she whispered, when he reached her breasts and sucked her nipple through her silk tank top. The pleasure was most exquisite.

Raking her fingers through his hair, she held him to her, quivering in delight as he gave a lusty groan. She arched her back when she felt his mounting desire, thrilled to know she had this affect on him. Warm and wanting, her body buzzed to life and she ran her hands over his shoulders, loving the way his muscles clenched and bunched beneath her touch.

The scent of her arousal perfumed the room, and she listened to Dimitri suck in sharp breath, as he sank to his knees, his mouth going to her stomach. He held her tight, and with excruciating slowness, moved his lips over her midriff, nipping her sensitive flesh with his teeth. As her passion soared, she gave a low groan of need, his slow, tender seduction nearly killing her.

He trailed his hands over her inner thighs, a slow lazy caress that left goose bumps in its wake. He paused before reaching the damp triangular patch that needed his attention, his eyes gauging her reactions. When her gaze met his, and she saw raw lust in his eyes, her sex fluttered, her breath leaving her lungs in a whoosh. They exchanged a long, heated look, her eyes conveying without words how much her body beckoned his touch, his mouth, his cock.

Taking charge of her pleasure, one hand slid higher and higher, and he didn't seem to be turned off by her chubby thighs. His hand stopped when he reached the lacey band of her panties. With one quick tug, he pulled them from her hips.

A strange, strangled noise came from the depths of her throat as he bared her pussy. Her entire body moistened, and when he growled in return, it made her feel so desirable, so sexy.

He fingered the soft material on her skirt, then bunched it into his hands. He leaned into her, his breath hot on her thighs as he parted her pink lips with his tongue. She gasped, a tremor wracking her body at that first sweet touch to her clit. Hot, and oh so wet, his swirled the soft blade of his tongue over her sensitive cleft, and she widened her legs, granting him deeper access as he took full possession of her pussy.

"So sweet," he murmured, his rich decadent rumble of pleasure curling around her. "So damn sweet."

Feeling wild, frantic and not wanting to hold anything back she let loose a breathy moan, her body craving so much more. "Please…" she begged.

"Is this want you want?" He pushed a finger inside her and fire whipped through her blood.

"Yes," she cried out, moving against his finger as basic elemental need took over.

"You are so responsive," he murmured as her body burned up with need. Another finger slid into her and he pushed deeper, slowly pumping into her as he raised her passion to never-before-known heights.

As his gifted her with long, luxurious strokes, her mind stopped working. No longer able to think, and only able to feel, she began to rock her hips, letting go of all inhibitions and moving against his mouth, her body shaking with an intensity that was both frightening and exciting.

Her pussy dripped with desire as he ravaged her, and their moans of pleasure blended. It shocked and thrilled her to watch Dimitri take joy in pleasuring her, and as she loosened, some working brain cell alerted her to the fact that she wasn't frigid, she just wasn't with the right guy—one who gave her confidence and encouraged her to embrace her body, just the way it is.

Sagging against the wall as he feathered heated kisses over her pussy, she succumbed to the pleasure. Her skin grew tight, and her insides quaked in a way that was unbelievably mind-blowing.

A barrage of sensations overcame her, and her body convulsed. God, she'd expected it to feel good, considering he was a guy who knew his way around a woman's body, but never had she expected it to feel this good.

As if sensing what she needed to take her to the precipice, he changed tactics, and roughly brushed his thumb over her clit. Her entire body trembled and burned beneath his artful manipulations.

"Look at me, Alexis," he commanded, and when she obeyed, the scalding heat in his eyes left her breathless. "Watch me taste you."

Eyes hazed with desire, Alexis watched as he delicately slid his tongue along the seam of her sex. Desire twisted inside her, her breath came in heavy, panting gasps.

She had never had an orgasm in her life, and honestly hadn't expected to have one with Dimitri, but with the way her body was tingling, her sex muscles clenching around his finger and her clit throbbing against his tongue, she was pretty sure she was about to have her first.

"It's good," she cried out, rocking her hips, desperate to feel the ultimate pleasure she'd only ever heard about. "So good."

Tension coiled through her and her eyes slipped shut as she vibrated from head to toe. He slipped one arm around her and absorbed her tremor as he continued to lick her, his fingers stroking deep inside. Then when he brushed his finger over something, something she assumed was the elusive G-spot that College Boy never bothered to find, she gasped and cried out his name. As bliss enveloped her, she fisted Dimitri's hair. Lacking any sort of discretion and giving no regard to the crowd outside the room, she moaned out loud, and pushed harder against his face.

Pleasure came sure and swift as the world around her closed in, nothing existing but this man and the delicious things his mouth and fingers were doing to her.

"Oh. My. God," she whimpered, the pleasure gaining momentum, building higher and higher, until her body finally let go with the hot flow of release. Coming apart like a piñata, moisture gushed between her legs. Dimitri growled, and stayed deep between her thighs, his tongue lapping gently as she rode out the pulsating waves.

She struggled to breathe, her chest still rising and falling as Dimitri climbed back up her body. He pushed his cock against her stomach as his mouth found hers. He kissed her deep and she savored the taste of herself on his tongue as he quickly unzipped his pants. She listened as he ripped into a foil packet, and once he sheathed himself he lifted her clear off the floor.

"Put your legs around me," he growled, the need and impatience in his voice making her feel so gloriously sexy and wanted as he pinned her against the wall. "I need to be inside you."

She nodded and he positioned his cock at her entrance. Holding her hips, he guided her down onto him. As he filled her, her head fell back, the fit so deliciously snug.

He buried his face in her neck and pumped into her, slamming into her so hard she feared they were going to go through the wall, but she loved the way he wanted her...needed her.

As he pushed open her tight walls and ravished her

with dark desire, she could once again feel soft ripples beginning at her core. Her nails dug into his back as she concentrated on the points of pleasure and when a second orgasm came out of nowhere, catching her completely off guard, her entire body shuddered. As her sex clenched around Dimitri's cock, he threw his head back and growled.

"I'm there, baby," he whispered. He drove all the way back in and stilled, his fingers biting into her hips as he released high inside her.

Her head dropped to his shoulder and they held each other for a long time, contentment singing through her blood. A little laugh welled up inside her, hardly able to believe what they'd just done, or how amazing she felt. Dimitri took deep labored breaths, then inched back to see her. He gave her a smile as he glanced over her face.

"I was wrong," he murmured.

"Wrong?" she asked unease moving through her.

He gave her a playful wink. "Yeah, you're very good at this." He brushed his thumb over her lips. "Damn good."

She laughed. "Maybe it's just because I was with the right guy."

He eased his cock out of her and she slid down his body. Loving the sexy way he made her feel, she stood there, wrapped in his arms, reveling in the things this man did to her, the way he made her feel. Her body tingled from head to toe, everywhere he touched still burning. A noise near the bar had her turning her head. She couldn't see into the darkness, but when she caught a very familiar scent, a knot of apprehension tightened her stomach.

Nikko...

Chapter Five

After only a few hours of sleep, Alexis kicked her sheets off and tossed and turned in her bed, her mind racing with unanswered questions.

Had Nikko been there last night?

Watching her?

As equal amounts of unease and excitement moved through her, she threw her legs over the side of her mattress and sat. Even though it gave her an unfamiliar rush to think he'd seen her with Dimitri, Alexis couldn't help but fear it could be the end of her summer job.

A quick glance at the clock told her it was midmorning, and since the patter of little feet hadn't woken her, she wondered if the others were up. She walked to her window, and put her hand over her stomach to suppress her nerves. How would she face Nikko this morning? Especially if he really had been there, watching.

She glanced out over the ocean and into Dimitri's backyard. When she saw Nikko standing there talking to him, her pulse jumped and she sucked in a quick breath. As if sensing her presence at the window, Dimitri lifted his head, a small smile on his face as their eyes met.

Oh. My. God.

Jerking back, Alexis pressed herself against the wall, praying they weren't discussing her and somehow knowing they were. She rushed to the bathroom and jumped into the shower to wash the scent of Dimitri off her skin. She stretched, her body aching in all the right places as memories of last night ambushed her. But now was not the time to think about all the things Dimitri had done to her, the way he made her feel so glorious, wanted…confident. No, now she had to figure out how she was going to face Nikko, and what the future held for her.

Once finished, she pulled on a demure sundress, one that hid her overflowing curves. Drawing a centering breath, and deciding to get this over with quickly, she opened her door, and made her way to the kitchen, fully expecting to find a pink slip waiting for her.

But when she found the house empty, not even the butler or housekeeper around, she frowned, and moved on through the house.

"Hello," she called out softly, padding quietly from room to room, anxiety building inside her.

She moved back to the kitchen, and Nikko's deep voice came through the intercom. "Please come to the pool deck, Alexis."

She swallowed against the tightness in her throat, and made her way down the winding staircase until she reached the sliding doors. She opened them, and stepped outside, the warm air washing over her body, but doing little to thaw the cold lump of dread forming in her stomach. Blinking against the bright rays, she spotted Nikko lounging at the table, a buffet of food spread before him. Sitting opposite him she found Dimitri, and when he popped a piece of fruit into his mouth, and then licked his fingers clean, her heart nearly stopped.

What is going on?

"Have a seat," Nikko said, his face expressionless.

She padded across the stone deck and lowered herself into the chair next to Dimitri. He shot her a smile, poured her a cup of coffee, and inched a tray of pastries toward her.

"What's going on?" she asked, wondering why Sophie wasn't having breakfast with her father. "Where is everyone?"

"The staff has the weekends off."

"Oh," she said. "And Sophie?"

"She spends the weekends with her grandparents." Nikko arched a questioning brow. "Did I forget to tell you that we have this place to ourselves on the weekends, Alexis?"

"Yes," she answered, her glance moving over the plates of delicious foods, but her stomach was too tense to eat. Something strange was going on here, and she wasn't sure what.

Nikko took a sip of coffee, and pushed back in his chair. He looked at her with those dark sexy eyes, and said, "We have a bit of a problem, Alexis."

Alexis felt her heart go into her throat, and when Dimitri shifted beside her, his warm beachy scent bringing back hot memories of last night it was all she could do not to moan. "We do?" she croaked out, her mouth going dry.

"Do you know who Dimitri is?"

"Your neighbor."

"Yes, but he's more than that. He's my business partner."

Oh God, this wasn't good, not good at all. She had no idea they were partners. But now that she thought about it, the signs were all there—both young millionaires, their summer houses next to each other likely for work purposes, both away all week at meetings—she'd just missed them. Regardless, whether she'd known it or not, she had crossed a delicate line. Getting involved with her boss's partner wasn't all that different than getting involved with the boss himself.

She stole a glance at Dimitri. His dark eyes held a bit of mischief as they locked on hers. "I had no idea," she said, wondering why he hadn't mentioned it.

"Dimitri and I, well…" Nikko tapped his forefinger on the table and looked at Dimitri. "Perhaps you'd like to tell her."

Dimitri took a bite of food, chewed slowly, and then began, "We split everything 50/50. It's what makes our professional relationship work so well."

"Okay," she said slowly, her glance going back and forth between the two, wondering what she was missing. What the hell did their business practices have to do with what had happened between Dimitri and herself the night before?

Nikko angled his head, his gaze moving over her face with a thoroughness that had her shifting in her chair. "It's also what makes our personal relationship work."

She sat there for a moment, mulling over the fact that they shared everything—professional and personal— while both men stared at her. Then understanding slowly dawned. Her body came alive, her blood pulsing hot. Surely to God she had to be mistaken. They couldn't be suggesting what she thought they were suggesting.

Could they?

"Are you saying…?"

Nikko stood and came around to her side of the table. He pulled her chair back. "We're saying we share everything, Alexis."

"Everything," she croaked out, when he grabbed her hand and helped her from the chair.

Dimitri stood and came up beside her. "Yes, love, everything." His hair fell into his eyes making him look so adorable as his gaze traveled the length of her. "And we both think a beautiful body like yours was made to be shared equally between us."

She looked at Nikko and saw real desire in his eyes. "You think I have a beautiful body?"

Nikko laughed. "Alexis, you've been driving me crazy. Wearing these dresses that hide your luscious curves. It's all I could do not to rip them from your body and give you the kind of attention you deserve." He dipped his head, his shrewd eyes moving over her face. "The kind of attention you came to Greece looking for."

"Oh…" she managed and looked at Dimitri. "You told him?"

"He didn't have to," Nikko said. "You communicate so much with your eyes, your body."

God, was she really such an easy read? "So you both knew one of the reasons I came here—"

"—was to learn the ropes," Nikko said.

She gulped. "There will be ropes?"

Dimitri laughed and piped in with, "If you like."

"And now that we have the place alone," Nikko began, trailing the rough pad of his index finger down her arm. "We were thinking we could both give you the hands-on experience you're looking for."

Her pulse leapt as she thought about these two men, sharing everything, sharing *her*, and having *four* hands on her body, two pairs of lips on her skin…She angled her head to see Nikko. "You were there last night weren't you?"

"Of course."

"You like to watch?"

"I like to do a lot of things."

Her glance tennis balled back and forth between the

two of them, confidence bubbling up inside her to know these two hot, gorgeous millionaires both wanted her. Feeling sexy and bold, she said, "Then why don't you show me?"

"Better yet," he began, his eyes darkening with lust as the air crackled with sexual tension. "Why don't *you* show us?"

"Show you?" she asked, wondering what he was getting at.

"This experience you're looking for," he said, as he gripped the hem of her dress. "I think you should use your own hands to start."

She gulped as she considered what he was suggesting. She'd barely touched herself when she was alone, and couldn't imagine doing something so intimate, so naughty in front of this captive audience of two.

"Yes, Alexis, touch yourself for us," Dimitri coaxed, his hot voice stroking her body in the most sensual way as Nikko fingered the material on her dress. She blinked up at them, uncertain, but when Dimitri said, "You need to learn your way around your body, Alexis, using your own hands. Only then will you understand and appreciate your curves the way we do."

Everything in the hungry way they were looking at her filled her with heat and prompted her into action. She gripped the bottom of her dress and pulled it over her head. When Nikko sucked in a sharp breath, genuine appreciation in his eyes, she could feel her nervousness ebb away.

His eyes dimmed with desire. "Don't ever hide yourself, Alexis. You are so incredibly beautiful."

They both stood there, taking their time to gaze at her near nakedness. Feeling a strange sense of power mushrooming inside her, she pushed her cleavage out a little more, never having felt so wanted, so desired.

Her fingers went to her bra, and she unhooked it from the back. It fell to the pool deck as her hands cupped her breasts. Loving the way the two were tracking her every movement, raw lust shimmering in their eyes, she brushed her thumbs over her nipples, enjoying the weight of her heavy breasts in her palms.

Want burned through her body when she let her hands slide lower. She wiggled out of her panties, and kicked them aside. She met Dimitri's glance, and as her body craved to feel him inside her again, she inched her legs open in invitation.

Nikko growled, ecstasy flitting across his face as she ran her hands over her soft swells. Enjoying the feel of her body for the very first time, she slipped a hand between her legs to touch her sex.

When she found herself damp with passion, her finger slicking along her slit so easily, she moaned out loud, the sound causing both men to move at once. Nikko's lips found hers, and she kissed him deeply, pulling his scent into her lungs as Dimitri pressed against her back, moving her hair to the side to run his lips along the back of her neck. A moment later his hands slipped around her body to play with her breasts, and Nikko's fingers joined hers between her legs.

"Oh, God," she moaned as they moved their masterful hands over her body. Need pumped through her veins, her skin flushing hotly as her libido roared to life.

She pushed her pelvis forward, rubbing up against Nikko's finger, and a low tortured groan crawled out of his throat. Heat spread over her skin when Nikko abandoned her mouth and kissed the hollow of her throat, going lower and lower until his lips found her breasts. He swiped his tongue over one hard nub, and intense pleasure gathered in her core.

"That feels so good."

She heard the soft rustle of clothes from behind as Dimitri undressed, then stepped back up to her. He gripped her hands and held them behind her back, forcing her chest out as Nikko licked and sucked her nipples. His burning mouth sucked greedily, alternating between both breasts like he couldn't get enough of her.

She moved against him, and gave a breathy moan as he inserted one long, thick finger into her dripping pussy. Her channel clamped around him and he bit down harder on her nipple. She cried out, and he shot her a glance before he sank to his knees. She moistened her lips as she watched him press kisses to the soft mound of her stomach, dipping lower and lower until he reached her sex. Her skin tightened beneath Nikko's mouth, and she sucked in a gasp when she heard the crinkle of foil ripping before Dimitri sheathed himself.

Nikko's tongue moved over her pussy. Her fingers curled in his hair, holding him to her, never wanting the moment to end, but when her knees wobbled, Dimitri caught her from behind.

Nikko rose to his feet, his eyes hot and heavy lidded as he steadied her. He looked over her head at Dimitri. "Lay her down."

Taking her hand, Dimitri led her to a richly padded lounge chair. Alexis throbbed with renewed excitement as he nudged her down and climbed onto the chair with her, hovering over her. The intimate look on his face took her breath away, told her how much he wanted her, how much he enjoyed her body.

"I need to be inside you," he said roughly.

"Yes, please," was all she could get out.

He widened her legs with his knees and positioned his cock at her entrance where he dragged the broad head through her wet folds. His bangs fell forward and she pushed them back as Nikko knelt beside her. Eyes full of want caught and held hers before his lips found hers. He kissed her deeply, his tongue slipping into her mouth as Dimitri pushed inside her pussy. The stab of pleasure was so intense, so incredibly mind blowing, she gasped into Nikko's mouth. Her thoughts scattered as they all shared intimacies, taking pleasure in each other's bodies.

Honestly, she wasn't the kind of girl who did stuff like this, but everything about it felt so right, so honest. Perfect. Everywhere they touched filled her with warmth, every ounce of insecurity gone, kissed away by these perceptive men, who only wanted to see to pleasure her, and to take theirs from her.

As her body joined with Dimitri's, she felt a surge of female prowess, and began moving against him, meeting and welcoming each hard stroke. Her heart raced, understanding there was something undeniably beautiful in being lavished and adored by these two.

Her hands went to her breasts to knead them, and when she whimpered for release, the two guys moaned in frank appreciation. The sweet sound of their ecstasy pushed her over the edge and her body began clenching around the cock inside her.

A moment later, she felt Dimitri swelling inside her, then he gripped her shoulders hard as he let go. Before she even had time to catch her breath, Dimitri rolled, positioned her on top of him on the lounge chair, her breasts squished against his chest. As she lay over his body, feeling a deep sense of satisfaction rolling through her, Nikko stepped over her and gripped her hips. He gave a tug until she was on her hands and knees. Eyes flaring hot, Dimitri grinned up at her from the chair below.

Nikko's hands slowly move over her back, introducing himself to her slowly as he shaped the swell of her backside.

"So damn gorgeous," he murmured, his soft voice

generating need inside her. She loved the way he wanted her, the way his body reacted to hers.

That thought had her throbbing all over again as their scents mingled and filled the air. Dimitri brushed her cheek with the back of his fingers, and an erotic whimper bubbled in her throat when Nikko sheathed himself and pushed into her slowly. Her entire body broke out in a fine sheen of sweat and she began moving against him, her body demanding more…*everything.*

As if sensing her needs, he picked up the pace, his hands moving over her back as he ravaged her.

Pleasure…so much pleasure.

Her body quivered as they all gave and took, and Dimitri swallowed her moan when his lips found hers. He kissed her as Nikko pounded into her, the onslaught of pleasure almost more than she could bear.

"I want you to come for us again," Dimitri whispered, a bone deep warmth moving through her as he reached between their bodies to rub her throbbing clit.

"Yes," she hissed, her breasts growing heavy, achy as the men took full possession of her body.

As soon as Dimitri applied pressure, a ripple moved through her, and her pussy clenched down hard on Nikko.

"Jesus," he growled. He leaned over her back, wrapped his arms around her waist and blew out a harsh breath as he let himself succumb to the pleasure.

When he stopped spasming, she collapsed on top of Dimitri, and Nikko collapsed on top of her. They stayed like that for a long time, just holding each other, and loving the comfortableness between them all.

Once their breathing returned to normal, Nikko pulled out of her, and after both men disposed of their condoms, Dimitri picked her up and walked toward the gorgeous pool overlooking the breathtaking ocean.

When he gave her a devious look she squealed.

"What are you doing?" she asked squirming in his arms.

"I need to douse the flames inside me, otherwise I'm going to have to take you again."

But before she could free herself, he jumped into the pool with her. She yelped, but the water felt so glorious against her heated skin. Nikko jumped in with them, then disappeared under the waves, only to reappear again at the other end.

He crooked his finger, his dark sexy eyes beckoning her over. She swam to him, and when she reached him, he gathered her into his arms, and planted a warm kiss on her mouth. She kissed him back, enjoying the flavor of his mouth. After a long thorough exchange, he inched back and slapped her bare ass.

"Come on. Let's eat."

With contentment coursing through her veins, yet feeling a little off kilter because she had no idea what happens next, she climbed from the pool. Nikko wrapped her in a big fluffy towel as he led her to the table. Dimitri slicked his long bangs back and sat next to them, completely naked.

"I'm starving," he said, going straight for the sweet pastries.

Alexis reached for a piece of fruit, her mind still spinning, trying to wrap itself around what had just happened and where the three of them went from here, when Nikko's hand closed over hers. The smile fell from his face as Dimitri put the delicious looking pastries in front of her.

"Eat, Alexis," Nikko said, as he plopped a piece of Danish into her mouth. "If we're going to fuck like this every weekend, you'll need your energy, and besides, I love your luscious body just the way it is."

She blinked the water from her lashes. "We're going to do this…every weekend?"

"Of course," Nikko said, tossing back a bite of icing

filled cinnamon roll. "Isn't that what you want?"

"Well…yes," she answered realizing she'd struck gold and how excited her best friend was going to be when she told her about this. Mel had always believed in her, and was the only one who made her feel good about herself until these two incredible men came into her life.

"Good, because it's what we want too." As she chewed, Nikko watched her. "Tell me why you would want to deprive yourself of food."

"The guys back home," she began and looked down at herself, "I was never good enough. I thought if I could slim down…"

"Haven't we already established that those guys are assholes," Dimitri said.

"And you've got it all wrong, baby," Nikko piped in, so much lust in his eyes as he looked at her. "They're not too good for you. You're too good for them."

As she popped another piece of Danish into her mouth and savored the sweetness, she stared at the two men who were gifting her with so much more than sex and food, certain she'd died and gone to heaven. Still unable to wrap her brain around this amazing turn of events, she reached for another sweet, but her towel slipped from her shoulders. She became acutely aware of her nakedness, and the way the two stopped eating, turning their attention to her.

Feeling a little sassy under their hungry gazes, she tossed a pastry into her mouth and moaned in bliss as she arched her back. As she teased them, she couldn't help but think maybe they were right, maybe if a guy couldn't appreciate her the way she was, then maybe he didn't deserve her at all.

But she couldn't think about that right now, not with the way Nikko was coming closer, his ravenous gaze latched on her breasts like they were more delectable than the plump, juicy strawberry he'd just popped into his mouth.

She let out a little yelp when he bit down on her nipple, and as the cool strawberry juice dripped down her flesh, Dimitri leaned in to lap it up. When she felt four hands on her, eager and ready to take her again, a new sense of confidence filled her and she knew beyond a shadow of a doubt, that this was going to be one hell of a summer.

EPILOGUE

With summer coming to an end, Alexis climbed from the water, and breathed in the tang of salty sea water drifting by in the breeze. Equal amounts of joy and sadness welled up inside her, knowing her time in Greece was coming to an end, but oh, what a time she'd had. She walked along the end of the pool, enjoying her last weekend at the mansion, as well as a plate of snacks and a cool glass of sweetened iced tea—extra sugar.

She wrung out her wet hair, and made her way to her lounge chair to where she found her lotion. Taking care to reapply after getting wet, she adjusted her bathing suit top, one of the many new—skimpy—suits she'd picked up over the last two months.

Lifting her leg, she balanced it on her chair and squirted a generous amount of lotion onto her bare flesh. She bent forward, taking her time to rub it in, slowly, carefully, making sure to coat every last inch the way Dimitri had taught her that first day on the beach.

A smile tugged at the corners of her mouth when she heard a deep guttural groan coming from the open office window overlooking the pool. Ignoring the sound, and loving the seductive game that she'd been playing with her two favorite guys over the course of the summer, she switched legs, taking care to stretch it out so she'd have to bend over further.

She heard the back gate open, and when Dimitri's unique scent curled around her, she didn't turn around to greet him. Instead, she ran her hands up her legs, her stomach, stopping only when she reached her breasts. She dipped her hands into her cleavage, and let loose a little moan as she touched herself, all the while pretending she hadn't noticed his approach.

She could feel him watching her, and it thrilled her to know how much he enjoyed it when she caressed herself, how much she herself enjoyed touching her own body. As she thought about her summer it occurred to her that she'd come to Greece looking for a hands-on experience, not to fall in love. But over the course of the summer, she went ahead and did just that. And the one person she'd fallen in love with was none other than herself. With the help of these two amazing men, she had learned so much about herself, and learned to love Alexis Cassidy, just the way she was.

A quiver moved through her as she ran her hands over her breasts, her stomach, her curvaceous backside, taking pleasure in stroking body.

"Hey," Nikko said stepping closer, his magnificent body crowding hers. "Need a hand."

Grinning, and feeling so completely sexy and wanted, she turned to him. As she stood before him wearing next to nothing, completely comfortable in her own skin, she murmured playfully, "I thought you'd never ask."

"Maybe she needs two," Dimitri said, stepping up behind her, pressing his hard cock to the small of her back as he sandwiched her between the two guys who rocked her world and turned her from a shy, inexperienced girl with body image issues, to a confident woman who knew what she wanted, and knew who she wanted it from.

They ran their hands over her body, and she exhaled a contended sigh as they began to pleasure her the same way they'd been pleasuring her all summer.

While there was no doubt that she'd had the time of her life in Greece, and she was sad to leave in a few days, she was also looking forward to getting back to college and seeing her best friend again.

Even though she hadn't lost the weight she wanted—and no longer cared to since she'd learned to love her curves—she'd certainly gained the bedroom experience she was after. Over and over again.

Except she no longer had any desire to prove she was good enough to get invited to the football parties, to be noticed by one of the popular boys. Honestly, the last thing cared about was garnering the attention of a self-centered college boy who couldn't see her, or appreciate her for the big, beautiful woman she was.

But she couldn't think about that right now. Right now all she could think about was these two men, and how they were currently laying her out on the lounge chair, ready to feast on her body, and pleasure her the way she deserved to be pleasured.